With Halloween safely behind her, and her alternating lovers James and Mitch agreeing to share her time, Queenie Hart has more attention to spare for her fledgeling baking business, Queen of Tarts.

That's lucky, for she has a brand-new challenge. Her irascible landlord, Oliver, has laid it upon her to invent and create twelve brand new and original tarts in his honour and to deliver them to him on Christmas Day.

Queenie is eager to begin, and Mitch is eager to assist, but life is busy and fallout from Halloween needs to be addressed. What with finding time to be with Mitch, trying to keep in touch with James, taming Ayesha the Terrible, sorting out Shane and Branok, finding out what Angel Petty did with a parcel, and dealing with seven bells with a mind of their own, Queenie barely has time to think. Christmas is coming and twelve new tarts take time to create. The last recipe is elusive. Queenie just hopes she can make the deadline.

This book is a work of fiction. Names, characters, places, and incidents either are products of the author's imagination or are used fictitiously. Any resemblance to actual events or locales or persons, living or dead, is entirely coincidental.

Queen of Tarts 3
The Twelve Tarts of Christmas
Copyright © 2021 Lark Westerly
ISBN: 978-1-4874-2318-6
Cover art by Martine Jardin

Published by eXtasy Books Inc

Look for us online at:
www.eXtasybooks.com

Queen of Tarts 3
A Fairy in the Bed
The Twelve Tarts of Christmas

By

Lark Westerly

DEDICATION

For all the inventive cooks out there — you know who you are!

Author's Note

Queen of Tarts 1 and 2 tell the story of how Queenie Hart, pastrycook and independent woman, found a new home at The Belfry, met her two lovers, Mitchell Kingsolver and James Stuart, and how she got to know her landlords from Porthwellian Tredennick as well as Branok and Gillan St Ives, the relatives her father avoids. The Halloween Ball solved some of her problems, and Queenie temporarily farewelled James and settled down with Mitch at The Belfry. End of story. Except—I knew there was more to tell.

Exactly what did Oliver, Queenie's irascible senior landlord, want Queenie to pay in rent? What would happen when Ayesha the Terrible came to live at The Belfry? What was the mystery of Kerensa's bells? Would Queenie get her photograph of James and a matching one of Mitch? Who was the hidden ancestor in her family tree? How would her life proceed now Halloween was over and the Caledonian Curse was gone for another year?

Queen of Tarts 3 answers these questions in suitably festive fashion.

Queenie, Mitch, and James first appeared in Queen of Tarts 1. Branok and Gillan St Ives and their family and the firm of Porthwellian Tredennick also appear in the Being Tamzin series. Flick Dark, Kris Peckerdale, and Peck Grene have all featured in the Fairy in the Bed series.

Queen of Tarts 3 is set in November and December 2021, but for the purpose of this book, the Covid 19 pandemic never happened. The tide times at Fiddle Bay may not be correct, but after all, Fiddle Bay exists only in my imagination.

Will Queenie and her men pop up again? Well, there's a heather-hound to meet and an organ to discover. James has still not been revealed to Shane and there's more to be learn about Queenie's painting, so who knows?

CHAPTER ONE: POST-HALLOWEEN DE-BRIEFING

Queenie Hart, November 1st, 2021

Queenie Hart woke on Monday to a slew of mixed feelings. The first of November might not be a festival or a momentous day to most folk, but to Queenie it always stood out as a yin-yang day of the good and the not-so-good.

On the side of the good, she could return from the place she called *Caledonia-on-my-Mind,* a mental space where a cranky and contentious Scotswoman took her over for the whole of October and clear through Halloween.

On the side of the not-so-good, she had to repair the damage her streams of fantastical cod-Scottish dialect might have done to her relationships with . . . just about anybody, really. She usually also had to look for a new temporary job and restore her finances after Caledonia-inspired spending sprees.

This year, things had been a trifle different. More than a trifle, really. The good and the not-so-good were also changed. The good was better. The not-so-good . . . that remained to be seen.

A move from Sydney to a renovated church just outside Fiddle Bay a couple of months earlier had allowed her to establish and expand her fledgeling baking business, Queen of Tarts. She had made new friends and found eager clients for her luxury tarts. Then October struck . . . but now she was safely out the other side.

She turned to regard the best thing of all about the good of the day. Her lover, Mitchell Kingsolver, lay beside her. He was still asleep, and she took her time to examine his face. He was a pixie man, a fairy, but apart from his perfect and un-blemished olive skin, he could easily have passed for human. He was tall and lanky, slim-hipped and long-limbed, with dark hair worn a little long and thickly lashed hazel eyes. His mouth was charming. Almost everything about him was charming, even his klutziness when dealing with technology.

Two things needed work to make him her perfect lover. One was his cat, Ayesha. Queenie had never met the creature, but she knew Ayesha was a grey ice queen, a fay feline who was also a phaser. She wasn't too sure what all that meant, except that Ayesha ruled Mitch with an iron paw, sometimes barely tolerating him, but still insisting that he let her set and keep her routine.

Ayesha was currently staying with Mitch's mother, Danna, who looked after her every October while Mitch was una-voidably unavailable.

Ayesha fiercely resented being sent to stay with Danna, but the other option was untenable. Mitch lived most of the time at a place he called the *pied-a-terre* at nearby Borrowdale Junc-tion. He ferried passengers in his mini-bus, Ethel, between the station and Oakengrove, the big house at Fiddle Bay. He also did deliveries for Fiddle-de-Dee, the Fiddle Bay supermarket. His third job was the one where he traded as The Fixer, help-ing people in the greater Sydney area out of problems that needed fixing *now*. That was how he and Queenie had met. She'd had to leave her unit in Sydney within twenty-four hours and move into The Belfry, the converted church where she lived now. No moving company would agree to help her at such short notice. The Fixer said he would, and he did. He had helped her repeatedly thereafter.

The Fixer loved eating tarts and seemed fascinated by the

variety and the possibilities. Queenie made her living by inventing and baking them. It was a match made in heaven—almost.

Ayesha was a problem that had to be solved.

The other difficulty was James.

James Stuart was the most beautiful man Queenie had ever met. He was also the reason Mitch was unavailable during October. James had auburn hair, grey eyes and a pale Celt's complexion. His penchant for wearing argyle sweaters and tartan pyjamas was regrettable, but she could work with that. She loved James dearly—as much as she loved Mitch.

They were devoted to her, but they had resented one another for years.

The two of them were working on a rapprochement, and Queenie knew they'd made a good start already.

Not that they could ever function as a *ménage à trois*.

That, Queenie thought, necessitated both men being present in the same place at the same time. Mitch and James never were.

How could they be when they were, in some sense, *the same* man?

Just like Queenie's, their Octobers took a left-hand turn into chaos.

James had explained it to Queenie in simple terms. Mitchell Kingsolver had been born as a normal pixie lad. He had a fix-it manifestation, not uncommon in his order, which meant he had the imperative to solve problems for other people.

When he was about twelve, he developed a manifestation personality . . . James. The pattern worked itself out over the next two years and since then the two men had co-existed, with Mitch presenting for eleven months of the year and James emerging on the first day of October and departing in the last few seconds of Halloween. They looked different. They had different accents, and they had different tastes and different desires . . . except that they both wanted Queenie.

James had told Queenie that. He was used to having to defer to Mitch for eleven months each year, but in the matter of Queenie he was *not* prepared to give in. He had, after all, met her first in the previous October. They had spent just a few minutes together, but to James, that was enough to establish a prior claim.

Queenie hadn't met Mitch until ten months later, but she had got to know him rather well — intimately, in fact — before he had to defer to James on the first of October.

James knew his other self was Queenie's lover. He'd been furious about that, but at least he was prepared to talk about it.

Mitch, on the other hand, had tied himself in knots trying to prepare Queenie for his absence in October without ever mentioning James' existence.

Now that Mitch had re-emerged, his attitude of denial had to change. It *would* change. It already was changing. Queenie was determined to have her tart and eat it too. Except that *she* was the tart. Figuratively speaking.

She wanted to kiss Mitch awake and enjoy the morning glory deferred for far too long, but before she could get started on her delectable pixie man, her phone rang.

Queenie gave a startled bleat, and then she turned round to grab her phone from the nightstand.

Mitch didn't get along too well with phones. If he woke before she got hold of it, he would try to help her. He might then end up conjuring the phone halfway to Ethiopia.

"Yes?" she said, more abruptly than she'd intended as she fumbled the pick-up.

A chorus of *Happy Birthday to You* hit her unprepared ears in stereo.

Queenie jerked the phone away and realised belatedly that it was a video call.

Of course . . . I knew they'd call.

Two faces, rarely seen but still beloved, beamed at her from the screen.

The song ended with a long and loud smooching sound, again rendered in stereo, as her parents kissed her virtually.

"Happy birthday, my darling," her mum said.

Absence made the heart grow *much* fonder where Queenie and her parents were concerned.

"Thanks, Mum." Queenie smiled with genuine affection. Her mother, Liberty Hart, wrote self-help books and spoke at seminars. Her dad, Shane, had taken early retirement but still plied his trade as a builder wherever he and Liberty happened to be. They had sold up and gone travelling when Queenie left home, just as they'd always intended.

There was no estrangement, and Queenie had always known there was no going back under the parental wings. She'd moved out in complete knowledge that she would now be on her own.

"Are you still in bed, Queenie?"

Oh-oh. It hadn't taken long for Liberty to start disapproving.

"I am," Queenie said. "Late night," she added, although she had no need to justify herself to her mother.

"Oh? Did you go somewhere nice, love?" That was her dad, the conciliatory half of the couple. Shane disliked conflict almost as much as Mitch did.

"I did. It was—"

The bed rocked a little as Mitch woke and reached for Queenie. He pulled her backwards into his arms with a murmur of pleasure.

"Queenie?" That was her mum again. "Are you having an earthquake?"

"No Mum. And yes, Dad—it was lovely. I went to a Halloween Ball in *the* most glorious costume," Queenie said.

"That doesn't look like your place," Shane said. As a

builder, he had an acute eye for architectural detail.

"Well, it is."

"Your landlady been remodelling? That looks like a fine job of plastering."

"No—oh! Of course, you didn't know! I've moved."

"Oh? Where are you now?"

Mitch kissed her neck, closing a possessive hand over one of her breasts.

Queenie suppressed a squirm. "It's a place called The Belfry, at Kirk Circle—near Fiddle Bay," she explained.

"Oh." Her dad sounded puzzled.

"Well, that's a problem," her mum said, a little crossly.

"Why? It's a lovely place. Nice people. The rent's *much* lower . . ."

In fact, she'd been allowed to live rent-free for her first three months.

"We posted your birthday present to your Mother Goose Lane address."

"Oops." That was indeed a problem, but she fought back. "I thought we agreed we weren't going to do birthday and Christmas presents anymore?"

Liberty had the grace to look sheepish. "We did—but this was just perfect for you with your interest in baking. We wanted you to have something nice. Maybe your landlady will forward it to you."

Pigs might fly.

"I'll check with her," Queenie said.

"You really might have told us you'd moved," Liberty said.

"We do like to know where you are, love," Shane said.

"Why? I never know where *you* are . . . unless you call and tell me. It's not as if you can drop in to visit." Queenie sighed, and she added hastily, "Sorry. I'm just—"

Mitch pressed against her with obvious and urgent intent.

Queenie hitched around and gave him a gentle shove.

He woke properly at that, sitting up and saying, brightly,

"Are you okay, my love?"

"Aye, I'm bonnie." Queenie caught herself as a remnant of Caledonia-on-my-Mind infected her speech.

Liberty said, stiffly, "Queenie, *must* you?"

Queenie frowned. On a wicked impulse, she held out her phone to Mitch. "I'm in a fix," she said. "Can you deal with it?"

"Anything for you, my love." Mitch juggled the phone the right way up. "Good morning," he said, beaming at the screen.

Mitch adored his own parents. It was another of the few things he shared with James.

Queenie settled back, hands behind her head, to enjoy the show.

Ye ken ye should deal wi' your ain messes . . .

Och, let Mitch do it. He lo'es to help.

She heard her mother say, "Excuse me — who are you?"

"My name is Mitchell Kingsolver," he said readily. "And I expect you're Queenie's mum and dad."

"Guilty as charged," Shane said.

"I'd love to meet you sometime and go for a beer or a coffee or whatever you choose, but today we have rather a lot on."

"A lot of what?" Shane sounded suspicious.

"We have campaigns to plan, and Queenie says we need to talk about my roommate, my mani-self, tarts, dogs, bats and potential babies. We're expecting someone to unward the belltower door this morning and before that we need to have breakfast and a shower. Before that we need to have one another. It's a matter of urgency."

He paused courteously, to allow Queenie's parents to respond. They didn't.

Mitch said, "So thank you for calling. Queenie will no doubt call you back when it's a little more convenient. Don't worry, she's well and beautiful and I hope she's as happy as she looks. I *will* take as much care of her as she'll allow.

Goodbye for now."

He stabbed at the end-call button and somehow flipped the screen, starting a cacophony of bagpipe music, left over from Queenie's brush with Caledonia-on-my-Mind.

Queenie held out her hand and he gave her the phone.

She ended the music and then she stared him down.

"*What* a performance."

Mitch said gently, "Too much?"

"No, my lovely Fixer. It was perfect. I love them and they love me, but this morning I just *can't* be dealing with the fall-out." She tossed the phone on the nightstand, rolled over and held out her arms. "Are you ready?"

"Always," he said, smiling. He rolled in and kissed her with enthusiasm. "Let's debrief."

"I debriefed . . . or rather, deknickered . . . last night, as you well know."

Mitch beamed at her, his beautiful hazel eyes sparkling with joy and desire.

Queenie responded by scrambling on top of him and sitting down, hard.

Mitch's eyes widened and darkened, and she smiled down at him. "It's been a while. See how long you can hold out."

"Longer than you," he said. He made a minute adjustment with his hips, and Queenie let out a yip of surprise.

"No fair!" she gasped. She tried to hold back, but Mitch was far too skilled, and she yelled fit to ring the rafters.

Mitch, possibly perceiving she was too shell-shocked to keep moving, flipped them over and urged her to lift her legs. He, too was in a hurry, and a few seconds later, he gasped and collapsed on top of her, breathing hard.

Queenie, agreeably squashed, licked his shoulder.

He kissed her sweetly. "Good morning, my own darling love."

"Good morning to you, too," she said cordially.

"Mitch . . ."

"Yes, I know. You want to say good morning to James. Go ahead."

"I shall." Queenie pulled his head down and she kissed him gently, thinking of her other almost lover, Mitch's second self.

She was unsure if he would hear her, although he'd said he *would* know, on some level, if she was thinking of him.

She whispered, "Guid morning to ye, my ain dear laddie. This kiss is all for you, with my dearest love." She kissed Mitch again, and then she added, matter-of-factly, "Mitch, may I have a mop-up?"

He said, "Coming up," and he handed her what she needed. He rolled off, but instead of getting out of bed, he pulled her gently back into his arms.

"Your dearest love?"

He sounded displeased.

Queenie said, "Yes. I promised him that. I promise you that, too."

She remembered, belatedly, that she'd held off saying *I love you* to Mitch when October loomed. She could say it now.

"I love you, Mitchell Kingsolver."

Mitch said, "You really can love us both?"

"I can. I do. Not exactly in the same way, but it's to the same degree. I love you two more than I've ever loved *any-one* . . . except maybe my parents . . . and that's a totally different thing." She snuggled against him.

She didn't thank him for his suggestion that she might say good morning to James, or for his acquiescence in being kissed as a proxy. As she'd told James, she would never ask permission or accept being managed by either of them. She would love both men . . . or neither.

She was tossing up whether to have breakfast or to invite Mitch to share a shower or maybe to enjoy a post-coital nap and an encore first, when her phone rang for the second time that morning.

She frowned.

"I hope that's not Mum and Dad again."

Mitch kissed her breast.

"It might be a client."

"Better get it, then."

Queenie reached behind her. "Can't reach."

Mitch shifted one hand, and the phone popped into Queenie's grasp.

Not Ethiopia, then . . .

"Multitasking now?" she said, laughing. She poked *accept* and attempted to get the phone to her ear. "Hello?"

"Greet you, Queenie," a pleasant voice said. She recognised it instantly as her youngest landlord, Androw Tredennick.

"Oh, greet you, Andy. What's up?"

"I'm not sure how to answer that. We wondered if you'd care to let us in. I've brought Oliver as promised, to deal with the belltower door."

It took a couple of seconds for Queenie to grasp the situation. When she did, she rolled away from Mitch in a hurry and bounced to her feet. "Wh-where are you?" she asked, as the bright patches of colour from the stained-glass windows bathed her naked form.

"Just outside The Belfry. You *were* expecting us?"

Queenie rolled her eyes at Mitch, who lay relaxed in her bed with his hands clasped behind his head. He looked utterly happy

You mongrel. You're enjoying this.

"Yes, but not necessarily so early."

"It's gone half-past ten, and the tide's low enough, so we came through," Andy said.

"Okay—right—give me a minute to get dressed, and I'll be with you," Queenie said. She ended the call and then she widened her eyes at Mitch. "Don't just lie there, Master Fixer—*do* something!"

"Anything for you," he said readily. He got out of bed, and Queenie took a few seconds to admire him before he double-tapped his wrist with the other hand and was suddenly wearing his working clothes of dull green shirt and khaki pants. "I'll make them tea while you have a shower," he said. He blew her a kiss. "Take your time, my love."

Queenie grabbed a plaid blouse and pinafore and scooted down the wide steps from the mezzanine bedroom, then into the bathroom.

So much for my plan to introduce Mitch to the delights of showering together.

So much for my decision that Oliver must *unward the door before he gets anywhere near my kitchen.*

She dived into the shower, turned on the water and grabbed a tablet of soap.

The soothing scent of milk and honey filled the stall, and Queenie sighed. The evening before, she had shared the shower with James. This soap was his—something his mother concocted—and he'd given it to her as a gift.

Sweet gesture or a way of keeping him in my mind?

One never knew, with James.

I'd be right joyful if ye were here with me, laddie . . .

Queenie hurried through her ablutions. Her blue towel was unaccountably missing, replaced by a big one with a preposterous design of red and purple palm trees against a sunset sky. James again.

Making sure I'll no' forget ye, my laddie?

She dried herself hastily, imagining his satisfaction. He'd never yet touched her naked body, but he was making sure his towel did.

Dressed and with her hair tied back in a damp tail, Queenie hastily kissed the gorgeous thistle pendant she still wore and tucked it inside her blouse. It was far too *OTT* for a morning at home, but she was loath to take it off. James had given it to her, with love from his mother.

She pondered the intricacies of accepting a priceless heirloom from a woman she had not yet met . . . Then she went to find out what was happening with her lover and her landlords.

Chapter Two: Porthwellian and Tredennick

Queenie Hart, November 1st, 2021

Queenie found the three men in the kitchen.

Mitch had got some chairs in from the main room, and he was in the act of pouring tea into the pottery cups that Oliver Porthwellian had left behind when he moved out of The Belfry some years before.

Queenie drew in a big breath and composed herself before stepping forth to greet Oliver and Andy.

"Dellion didn't come?"

Dellion was Andy's wife, a lively pisky woman with whom Queenie had struck up a long-distance friendship. As a fairy woman, she had given Queenie invaluable advice about navigating the byways of romance with fairy men.

"No—she's wrangling our boys and minding the office, but she *will* come to see you someday soon," Andy said. "This is from her." He closed the gap between them and gathered Queenie into a warm hug. The unexpected and delightful scent of popcorn enveloped her.

Mmm . . . I can see why Dellion loves to snuggle with him.

He disengaged, stood back and held out his hand to her. "*Nos da*, Queenie. Mitchell has been bringing us up to speed on the status of the bats."

"I see." Queenie accepted his hand, just as if he'd not just cuddled her. She was learning all about the fairy idea of proxies.

She looked her youngest landlord over with interest. At twenty-six, Androw Tredennick was, in his own words, a very junior partner in the firm of Porthwellian Tredennick. He was a beautiful man, wearing silver buckles and buttons to proclaim his pure pisky heritage. The short earring in his left ear and a silver ring on his left hand proclaimed his married status, while the two silver rings on his right hand proclaimed him as the adoring father of two small sons.

Piskies had a reputation for being somewhat devious and difficult, but Andy had never been anything less than kind to her since she had first called him on her cousin's advice to discuss moving into the converted church.

The Belfry was one of many properties the firm of Porthwellian Tredennick administered. It stood apart from the others in that Oliver Porthwellian, the senior partner, had a personal interest in its welfare. He had lived there for some years, and he was most particular about who he allowed to move in. He was also most skilled in getting tenants to leave if they disappointed him.

A harrumph to her left drew Queenie's attention to Oliver, who was clearly fed up with waiting for her to notice him.

Oliver Porthwellian was ninety-six, but he could have passed for a man in his early seventies. He was as slim and upright as his great-grandson-in-law. His face was handsome and austere, but the raffish set to his mouth hinted at the other side of Oliver—a side that scandalised even the broad-minded Dellion.

Her wails of *Granddad!* came to Queenie's memory, making her grin.

"Hello, Oliver," she said cordially. She'd been late with his order of luxury tarts the day before, but she wasn't going to apologise for that. Yesterday had been a busy day, spent creating memories with James, going to the Halloween Ball, and negotiating the handover when it was time for James to say goodbye.

She offered her hand.

Oliver rose from his chair with alacrity. He took Queenie's hand, bowed over it, and gave her a smart once-over.

Queenie waited with interest for his opening salvo. He was quite capable of throwing a hissy fit about the tarts. He was also quite capable of making an inappropriate comment to her or about her.

According to Andy, Oliver knew perfectly well how to behave in public. He just didn't always choose to.

Nothing happened.

"What, mun, nae wee comment aboot the size o' ma titties or the breadth of ma bahooshie?" Queenie asked.

Oliver's eyebrows rose just a little. He snapped his head around to peer at Mitch, making his short silver earring jingle.

Then he turned back to Queenie. "This is not the laddie you were snuggling up to last week," he stated.

"Not exactly."

As you know fu' weel.

"Yet he informed us he was present when the bats departed from the belltower in the early hours of this morning."

"He was. And to be accurate, I wasn't snuggling with James last week."

"He had his arm around you."

"He was encroaching on me."

"You weren't objecting."

Queenie widened her eyes at him. "Why on earth would I object to that? He's a beautiful braeside laddie and he smells delightfully of clean wool. He came to the Halloween Ball with me last night, and we made promises. He's gone now. Mitch is here instead, and he's every bit as cuddly and sweet-smelling as my Jamie. Aren't I the lucky one?"

Oliver gave her a wintery smile. "You are, I do believe. What have you done with your razor-tongued lassie? I saw a glimpse of her just now, but at the moment you sound — human."

"I *am* human. Mostly. Lassie Haggis is still here though, as you weel know, thou impertinent mannie . . . but since October is done for the year, I am able to keep her civil and quiet . . . unless I'm pushed a wee bit too far by an evil auld pisky mun."

Oliver inclined his head. "Then I'll take care not to push you too far. You might threaten again to withhold my tarts."

"I won't do that ever again. Yesterday's omission was an oversight. Mitch will make sure I remember next week."

She hoped so, anyway. Mitch's system of using his collection of caps as his engagement diary was something she had not yet managed to fathom.

"Very good." Oliver glanced at Mitch again, then back to Queenie. "Have you a kiss for an evil old man?"

"No. But I have one for *you*, dear Oliver." She reached up on tiptoe and kissed his cheek. He smelled agreeably of grapefruit. All the fay Queenie had so far knowingly met had their own personal scents. They called these their *bouquet-des-fees*.

Even she seemed to have a faint one, courtesy of her unexplained trace of fairy blood. She knew this came from an ancestor on Liberty's side of the family, but Liberty didn't know who it was.

Liberty must have had more fay blood than Queenie, but as far as Queenie knew it had never presented itself.

"Thank you, my dear." Oliver gave her a formal hug, kissed her cheek, and subsided into his chair. He turned his attention to Andy, who was watching with undisguised enjoyment. "As I have told you from the beginning, Androw, Miss Hart is the perfect tenant for The Belfry. I think we need not wait for the initial term to end. We should ratify her circumstantial lease immediately."

Without waiting for an answer, he snapped his fingers, and

16

a yellow envelope appeared on the table. "Look this over, my dear, and if you're satisfied with the terms, we can sign it today."

Queenie took the agreement. She had taken The Belfry for an initial rent-free three-month period in mid-August. That period would be up in another two weeks. She was aware that if and when she renewed the lease, she would be obliged to pay a peppercorn rent . . . or to provide payment in kind.

She had been doubtful about agreeing to that, but her long-distance acquaintance with her landlords had been positive so far. Besides, her dad's cousin had recommended them. There was no love lost between the half-pisky Branok St Ives and his wholly human cousin Shane Hart, but Branok's personal code of ethics would not allow him to take it out on Queenie.

She said to Mitch, "Would you get some tarts and shortbread out, please? I'll read this through."

Mitch fetched out a selection of tarts and butter shortbread, and he and Oliver set to work on them. Andy ate one tart with apparent enjoyment, but then he returned his attention to Queenie.

"It is negotiable," he said.

"Wheest," Queenie said absently. She was longing to watch Mitch eat. Watching people eat was one of her favourite things, but for now she had to pay attention to her paperwork.

The agreement was short. The terms were as before, except she no longer had to ask before making cosmetic changes to her home. Major structural changes were still to be cleared personally with Oliver Porthwellian *while I am above ground. After that, you may do as you please. Androw and Dellion have agreed to this.*

Queenie got to the clause about the rent and read it through.

She had wondered what the firm might consider as an

appropriate ongoing rent. Now she knew.

She raised her head and looked at Andy. "Are you sure this is right?" She tapped the clause.

Andy shrugged. "I would suppose so. Oliver drew it up."

Oliver bit into an apple jelly Adam and Eve tart. "Superb," he said. "Please add three of these to my next order."

"Which ones should I take out?" Queenie asked.

"None. I did say *add*, not *substitute*. The order will henceforth contain fifteen assorted tarts, plus a dozen of your excellent shortbreads . . . thistle print preferred."

"My mistake," she said. "We may have to invest in a bigger tureen." She held out her hand. "Mitch, may I borrow your pen?"

Mitch handed her his fountain pen. It was made of polished wood—possibly bamboo, and he always had it with him . . . excepting the time he'd left it with Queenie by mistake. Or possibly on purpose.

Queenie signed and initialled the agreement, and then she pushed it over to Mitch, who put down one of his favourite Ruby Tuesday tarts to sign as witness, adding a smear of jam in the process.

Queenie returned the agreement to Oliver, who conjured his own dip pen and signed in his turn. Andy countersigned as witness, and Queenie sighed with pleasure.

In two weeks' time, she would have the right to live in The Belfry for as long as she chose . . . so long as she paid her rent.

Chapter Three: Unwarding the Door

Queenie Hart, November 1st, 2021

"I trust the terms of the agreement seem fair?" Oliver asked belatedly. He embarked on a Currant Affairs tart, made with black and red currants sent by Mitch and James' mother.

"They're more than fair," Queenie said.

"Equitable," Oliver corrected. "You get what you want, and I get what I want. This one is very good, but it needs a little lemon juice to stabilise the flavours."

"Thank you. I'll adjust the recipe." Queenie took a tart for herself. She was about to pour her tea when Mitch did it for her. She noted that he'd used the tealeaves James preferred rather than teabags, and she blew him a kiss.

Twenty minutes later, Oliver dusted off his fingers on a fine white handkerchief. He had consumed at least half a dozen tarts and three pieces of shortbread, but he still managed to look aesthetic and austere. He got to his feet. "Time's a'wasting," he said. "Time to open that door." He headed off towards the narthex.

Queenie drained her teacup and followed.

For the past month, she been disturbed by odd flutterings inside the belltower. At first, she'd put it down to the black birds who lived in the dark trees near the old graveyard. It had grown rapidly worse, until late one night, she'd been so unnerved that she'd broken her self-imposed October isolation and telephoned the Fixer number.

Mitch had been unavailable, and James had turned up instead, startling Queenie considerably. He wasn't a Fixer, but he'd done his best to investigate the disturbance before conceding defeat. He thought the creatures in the belltower were fay bats, but he couldn't open the door to check because it was warded shut.

Oliver had admitted to importing the bats *and* to warding the door, but he'd said the bats would leave on their own after All Hallows. Leave they had, flitting away through the cave that led to *over there,* the fay homeland, where they would stay until next October.

The door, presumably, remained obdurate.

Queenie overtook Oliver and made a last attempt to open it, pulling and shoving the door. She was tempted to give it a good battering with her newly acquired besom, but she thought better of it. Oliver might construe that as structural changes and threaten to evict her.

The door was undoubtedly stuck.

Mitch hadn't been available to try fixing the situation, but now that Oliver was here, the question was academic.

Oliver stepped up to the door, a sturdy wooden one with a loop of coarse rope instead of a handle.

He laid one elegant hand flat on the door.

Then he stepped back. "It's done."

Well!

Queenie felt her eyebrows rise into her hair.

"Now, we'll be off," Oliver said.

Andy held up his hand. "Not yet, Oliver. I promised Queenie I'd send you up into the tower first to check for stragglers."

"There won't be any." Nevertheless, Oliver turned to Queenie. "You do the honours, my dear."

Queenie grabbed the rope. She tugged sharply. Nothing

happened.

"No, you need to coax it," Oliver said. "Turn it gently ninety degrees right, and then the loop will engage with the mechanism and the door will open."

Queenie tried. The rope, so recalcitrant since she'd come to live at The Belfry, turned sweetly in her hand. The door swung open in silence.

"What, no theatrical creaks?" she enquired.

Oliver ignored that. He stepped past and mounted the steep steps that spiralled out of sight into the tower.

He must have conjured a torch, for the dancing light flashed among timbers, ropes, and the bronze of seven bells.

Queenie heard him moving about and perceived the very soft ting of the bells in response to the vibration.

"Are the wee beasties all gone?" she called.

"Every whisker has departed on schedule," Oliver rejoined. He came down the steps. His face was melancholy. He stopped in front of Queenie. "You may now go up there whenever you like, although I recommend you desist from doing so in October.

"Feel free to clean, sweep and dust—or not. If you do choose to clean up, I'd be obliged if you polish Kerensa's bells. However, you're under no obligation to do that."

"I expect I shall," Queenie said. "Is it very dirty?"

"Not too bad, considering." Oliver gave her an unrepentant grin. "I'll send you five gross of sacks for the guano. You might sell some along with your excellent tarts."

"Oh, might I," Queenie grumbled, but she managed a pleasant smile for her departing landlords. "Where's your car?"

"Back at the St Botolph's Church gateway," Andy said. He must have seen Queenie didn't understand, for he elaborated, "We drove to the old gateway church and went through to *over there*. Then we came here through the cove gateway."

"It doesn't get any easier," Oliver observed. "Bending double under a rock slab and facing rogue waves and seaweed and concealed dips is no longer conducive to my health and temper."

Queenie recalled she'd been told he'd initially left The Belfry because the walk to the office was becoming arduous. Since the offices of Porthwellian Tredennick were a thousand kilometres away from Fiddle Bay, she'd thought he must have meant a local office.

Clearly, he hadn't.

"Never mind, Oliver. The tide will be low enough to get back," Andy said. "You get going. I want a word with Queenie."

"I'll drive you to the cove if you want," Mitch said.

Oliver peered at Ethel, the green mini-bus Mitch used for his various occupations. "Very well," he conceded. He mounted into the bus and settled in the seat. "Coming, Andrew?"

"I'll walk," Andy called.

Oliver blew a kiss to Queenie. "Take care of yourself, my dear." He waited a beat, then he added, "By the way, I have appropriated the rest of the tarts from the table. That will save you from needing to put them away."

"Of course you have," Queenie said. "Goodbye, Oliver."

When the bus had departed, Andy turned to Queenie. "He didn't mean it about the guano."

"He didn't?"

"No. Undoubtedly there was some, but fay bats aren't as messy as the ones *over here*. I'm sure Oliver took care of it while he was checking the bells. He will be perfectly aware that your lungs might not be impervious to airborne particles."

"What *is* it with those bells?" Queenie asked.

"It was before my time, but apparently, the original ones

had been taken out and relocated or melted down when the church was deconsecrated," Andy explained. "Kerensa, Oliver's minx, was a bellfounder. She cast new bells for the tower. They all have names imprinted in the bronze, I believe."

"I see. Then they must be verra dear and verra personal to Oliver."

"I expect so. He and Kerensa lived here for a good many years, but when she went to glory he—he hadn't the heart to stay." His voice shook slightly. Maybe he was thinking it couldn't be too long before Oliver must follow his beloved wife.

He reached for her hand and gave it a companionable squeeze. "He's truly pleased that you've accepted the circumstantial lease, Queenie. He's a cantankerous old man, but he's fond of you. He also respects you."

"He has a verra odd way of showing it."

"He did try to rattle you, but you tossed it right back at him. No doubt he's currently giving Mitchell an earful about making sure he treats you well. How are you travelling with the manifestation problems, by the way?"

"The Caledonian Curse is gone, for the noo."

"Almost." Andy grinned.

"Don't make me take ma besom to you, wee mannie."

"You promised not to."

"So I did."

"How about the *other* mani problem?"

Queenie perceived Dellion must have reported on one of their private conversations. Fair enough. Andy *was* her husband.

"So far, so weel," she said. "James left me at midnight—midway through a kiss."

"And you thereby greeted Mitchell into a loving embrace," Andy said.

Queenie nodded. Apart from his slightly pointed ears and plethora of silver, Andy *looked* human.

That comment went to prove he wasn't. She tried to envision *any* human male of her acquaintance producing that with a straight face.

"Tell Dellion I'm taking her advice," she added.

"Which bit?"

"The both-or-neither bit, mainly. They're not keen to share me, but they like the alternative a lot less."

"Then your method of farewell and greeting was intended to set the pattern."

"It was, and I believe it worked. It's early days for us all, but I think we'll be all right."

"I think you'll be superb."

"Andy, would you be willing to share Dellion if it was the only way to be with her?"

He looked startled. "I think I must plead the fifth on that."

"I don't think we have a fifth in Australia."

"Then we ought to. I think . . . I *hope* . . . I could have brought myself to agree, but I can't be certain. Fortunately, the proposal was never made."

Queenie surveyed his face . . . sensitive and beguiling . . . He *looked* like an aesthete, but she was absolutely sure he and Dellion shared a passionate and highly physical relationship.

Andy cleared his throat. "I'm glad you're okay. Dellion will be, too. Discretion isn't her most obvious trait, but don't worry about her telling your business to anyone else. She shared it with me because I asked her if you would be all right. She said she'd tell me, because she wanted my attention solely on her and our sons. She will tell no one else, because no one else knows there's anything to ask."

He kissed her cheek as Oliver had. "Bye, Queenie. No, don't come with me. Go on in and let The Belfry know you're going to stay. It *will* try to claim you."

"I know. I'll allow that."

He looked up at the tower for a moment, then he turned and walked off.

Chapter Four: The First Tart

Queenie Hart, November 1st, 2021

Mitch was back at The Belfry within half an hour. "I waited with the old man until Andy got there," he said.

"Thanks," Queenie said. "Mitch, would you like to shower with me?"

"But you said—"

"I know what I said. I already had a shower, and I told you I didn't share, but the thing is, I let James wash my back. You do *know* that, right?"

He bit his lip.

"You know it and you accept it. What you might not know is that I started daydreaming about showering with you . . . I *want* you to come in with me, unless you'd rather not."

"In that case, I accept. Do you want to go back to bed first? To make it worthwhile showering again?"

"Yes, please."

They walked up the stair together, and Mitch got naked without her having to ask. Queenie stripped off her blouse and pinafore.

"You weren't wearing knickers," Mitch observed, raising one eyebrow.

"No. I had to dress in a hurry."

"You had two strange men in the kitchen, and you weren't wearing knickers."

"That's right. Not that they're all that strange." She stared at him, waiting to see where he was going with this.

Mitch said, "I must be a bit more perverse that I thought. I find that a wee bit exciting."

"You'd like me to put the pinafore back on?" Queenie asked.

"Would you mind?"

"Not a bit." She put it back on, dispensing with the blouse.

Mitch sighed contentedly. "Maybe you could just be bending over, straightening the bed, and I could surprise you."

"Maybe I—"

He pounced.

Queenie squealed.

It was wonderful.

When they were standing under the shower, washing off the morning's exertions, Mitch asked, "Queenie, if you don't mind me asking, what rent do you have to pay? I know what I pay for the *pied-a-terre,* and I'd like a comparison."

"It's not *rent,* exactly." She told him the terms she'd agreed to.

"Let me get this straight. Master Oliver Porthwellian has laid it upon you to invent twelve new and original tarts by Christmas *this year.*"

"Aye, and I have to remit the whole dozen to him on Christmas Day. He promises not to go to glory before then if he can possibly avoid it."

"He'll avoid it. I wouldn't be surprised if you're still making tarts for the old reprobate when he scores his century. But twelve new tarts? That's all?"

"Just about. Except that I'm no' to sell them to anyone else while he lives."

Mitch looked dismayed. "Does that mean I won't get to taste them? *Queenie!* How shall I bear it?"

"No, of course is doesnae mean that," Queenie said. "You can have whatever tarts you want, whenever you want. I'm the Queen of Tarts, remember, and what I say, goes."

"Excellent." Mitch sounded relieved. "What are the new tarts going to be like?"

"So far, I've thought of just one of them."

"Tell me *all* about it. In detail." An unmistakable greedy note came into Mitch's voice.

Queenie squirmed with pleasure. She adored talking tarts, and Mitch was always an avid accomplice. James—not so much. James preferred her shortbread.

"Okay. It's going to have chequerboard pastry, nicely browned, to represent the stone o' the belltower. It's going to have a burned caramel filling to give it a butterscotch note, a fine glaze, and it will have flecks of the best eighty-percent bitter chocolate suspended in the glaze."

Mitch moaned with anticipatory greed. "Oh, *Queenie.* I can't *wait.*"

"Ye'll hae to . . . I'll need to perfect the recipe."

"I'll be your tester. May I *please* be your tester?"

Queenie had an unwelcome flashback to the last time he had pleaded with her, when he begged her to let him explain . . . back in the last fraught days of September. She had hardened her heart against him.

I will never *do that again.*

"Naturally, you will be my tester," she said.

"Ahhhh. And what are you going to call that one? You know how important names are to the full tarting experience."

Queenie knew how important they were to Mitch, at any rate. It was he who had rechristened her plain starter tarts—the ones she used to test the oven setting—so they were now called Ruby Tuesdays.

She held out her hand for the soap.

Mitch gave her a slab that was a pale coffee colour. This must be the nut butter soap that his mother also made.

It wasn't the milk and honey recipe James liked best, but

she saw that at least Mitch hadn't removed that one from the shower stall.

Well, she was about to find out what Mitch liked best—aside from the Queen of Tarts and her wares.

She started soaping his chest, and the warm scent of almonds tickled her senses. She moved her hands down, and down.

Sharing a shower was rather delightful. She wondered why she had always rejected the idea before yesterday.

"If you go on doing that, something unfortunate might happen," Mitch said, as her hands slid rhythmically over his package. Despite their exertions—was it four or five couplings already today—there was a definite stirring . . . a rearing up . . . an anticipatory probing in the air.

"Och, let it happen." She went on with her ministrations. "By the way," she added as his breath hitched, his hips jerked, and his eyes widened with imminent explosion. "I'm calling the caramel and chocolate tart Bats in the Belfry."

Mitch moaned . . . for all the right reasons.

CHAPTER FIVE: THE AYESHA CONUNDRUM

Queenie Hart, November 5th, 2021

Queenie realised that she and Mitch had never actually discussed whether he would move into The Belfry with her.

James had the intention of spending most of his days and every night of his precious October with her next year, but he hadn't known — or possibly cared — what Mitch would want to do with his much more generous allotment of eleven months.

It was five days since Mitch's return. Queenie now had two framed photographs on her nightstand. One showed herself and James, arrayed in their Halloween finery. James looked heartbreakingly handsome in his Stuart kilt — the kilt of a *man grown*, which he had worn especially for Queenie. Queenie herself looked spectacular in her Queen of Tarts costume mid-calf at the back, short at the front, made from red, blue and gold brocade and silk and embroidered with magical designs by a fairy embroiderer. The statement pendant glowed above her cleavage.

Queenie acknowledged that she looked better than she ever had in that gown, and yet, looking into her pictured eyes, she saw a hint of *otherness* there.

Och, of course — that's her *— James' October lassie . . . Lassie Haggis.*

A shiver ran down her spine as she looked into her

pictured face and saw other eyes gazing out of her.

The second photograph was one of her with Mitch. For that one, she had chosen to wear her grey tunic with a soft green blouse, picked to tone with the gum-leaf shade Mitch often wore. She had posed theatrically with James, but with Mitch she'd been photographed seated in his lap, with her arm draped around his neck.

They'd used the same dark background and the same chairs, but everything else was different saving the thistle pendant. For some reason, Mitch had wanted that to be visible, and so she had agreed.

Well, it *was* a gift from the men's mother, Danna Kingsolver, and both Mitch and James undoubtedly adored their mother.

Another point in common . . .

Both photographs had been taken by Maureen Tucker, one of the editors of the local *Stradevarious* magazine. If she found it odd that Queenie wanted to be photographed with two different men in two days, she kept quiet about it. Maureen was sharp but tolerant, and she knew the value of minding her own business.

The prints were housed in a double frame of polished wood. Mitch had given it to her, and she hadn't enquired as to its provenance.

Every night and morning, Queenie kissed James' smiling face.

Mitch made no comment about that, but he made the effort to act as James' proxy when Queenie wanted to reconnect with her almost-lover.

It was an odd experience, because the two men kissed differently, and whichever one acted as proxy for the other held back his own response as well as he could.

On their fifth morning together, Queenie, lying in Mitch's arms in post-loving bliss, introduced a subject she'd been expecting *him* to tackle.

"Mitch, when are you going to fetch Ayesha?"

He'd been kissing her neck, and she felt him freeze.

She waited for a few seconds, unwilling to push the issue. He said, "I suppose . . ."

"There's no suppose about it, my love. You have a responsibility to her."

"I have." To his credit, he didn't point out how she'd objected to that in his last days before James took over.

"What are you going to do?" she asked.

"Do—"

"Aye, *do*. Yon moggy—" She broke off. "I mean, Ayesha will be expecting to move back into the *pied-a-terre* with you and go back to ruling you there."

"She will," he said.

"Is that what's going to happen?"

He stayed silent for so long she thought he wasn't going to answer, but then he said, "Ayesha is going to have to change her ways—or at least submit to having her routine adjusted. I can't and I won't risk losing you, darling Queenie."

"You won't lose me. As I see it, you have a few options open to you. You can move back to the *pied-a-terre* with her and come to me for horizontal dessert when it's convenient."

Horizontal dessert was a term Dellion Tredennick used, and Queenie had adopted it.

Mitch made a sound of protest at that.

"Or you can leave Ayesha with your mum, if she's willing."

"She would be willing, but—"

"But it's no' her responsibility," Queenie put in.

"It's not. I can't avoid having her look after her in October, because . . ."

Queenie understood. Ayesha detested James, and one of her attacks had left him permanently scarred. James detested her right back, but he had told Queenie he didn't wish her any harm. Queenie believed him.

"It's not October now," she pointed out. She continued, "If you want to keep living in the *pied-a-terre,* it need not be forever. James said she had an allotted span. Just how long *do* fay cats live?"

Mitch said, "A bit longer than cats this side of the gates, I think. Sixteen years or so at least."

"Longer than James' Horace, then."

"Yes." Mitch said sadly. "Ayesha hated Horace, too. It was unjust of her. He was a lovely dog. He never held it against me that I kept him from his master for such long stretches."

"Did he know?" She had hesitated to ask much about Horace of James, because he still sincerely mourned his deerhound.

"He knew, all right. He was always friendly to me. I'd have gladly looked after him, except for Ayesha."

"I see. You couldn't risk having her attack *him.*"

"No. Fortunately, he was happy with Georgie."

Mitch's cousin Georgiana had cared to Horace for eleven months of the year.

"Just how did you happen to have Ayesha?" Queenie asked. She knew Georgiana had given Horace to James, but she'd also gathered that Mitch liked dogs and wished he could have one. Instead, he was manipulated by his cat.

"She's the legacy of a Fixer job," Mitch said. "About six years ago, I got a call from a pixie miss living this side of the gates. She'd been given a kitten by one of her human friends. It was a stray. She'd taken it in but then she and her man had a child."

"Oh."

"Yes. She was in terror lest Ayesha harmed the baby. She hadn't so far, but the miss told me she'd caught her *looking* at the little lad and making a . . . a *high croon,* was the way she put it . . .and flexing her claws. She was desperately afraid, but she couldn't abandon Ayesha, and nor could she, in good conscience, give her away without warning the new owners."

"But where did she come from? What was a fay kitten doing *here*?"

"Not here—in Sydney. It seems likely she'd wandered through the castle bridge gateway—or maybe her mother had. The miss hadn't realised what Ayesha was until she realised she was a phaser."

"Yes, what is that? James mentioned it."

"It's a manifestation—some fay cats have it. It means they can't be confined. It's also sometimes called the Schrödinger manifestation, because even if you shut one in a box, which is a bad idea anyway, you can never be sure whether it's still there."

"I see. I think. So, you agreed to fix the problem."

"Yes. I brought her home. She resented me, but she deigned to stay. She's been with me ever since."

"Except when it's James' turn."

"Yes."

Queenie considered. "How old was she when you got her?"

"The miss thought she was about eighteen months."

"In that case, she's seven or eight now . . . and might live another eight or nine years."

Mitch said, "That's about right."

"Well then . . . that means you could stay at the *pied-a-terre* for another eight years."

"I don't want to do that."

"I don't want it, either, but it *is* a possibility. The only other thing I can think of is to have her move in here. She would still have to go to your mother when James is here, but that can't be helped."

Mitch said, "I don't know if that would work."

"Neither do I. But it *does* let you live with me, as long as that is what you want."

"It is."

"You're the Fixer. What would you advise someone else in this situation?"

"I did advise someone else . . ."

"And you ended up in the same situation, except that she *actually* harmed your other self instead of *potentially* harming a child. Well then. What do you think of this? You go and get Ayesha from your mum and bring her back here. Is there any way you can communicate with her?"

"No more than with any other cat. I suspect she's at least as clever as Horace was, but Horace, bless him, *wanted* to understand. He also wanted me to know he quite liked me."

"Cats like their owners, don't they?"

"I'm sure some do, but Ayesha doesn't see me as her owner. I don't know exactly what she does see — possibly a servant. Mind you — she was found by a human woman, adopted by the pixie miss, and then *I* took her, so she might even see me as her kidnapper."

"A cat with Stockholm syndrome."

"I doubt it." He added, "I think you had better come with me. That way, we can see how she reacts to you. I will *not* risk having her hurt you. And, before you ask, she has never shown any inclination to hurt my parents."

Queenie rolled around and kissed him. "Then let's do that today. You go and meet the train, and I'll get the day's orders done. Then I'll walk to the post office around one-thirty. Will that work?"

"That will work," Mitch said.

Queenie got out of bed and dressed in her tartan blouse and pinafore. She spent the morning making tarts, and she delivered some of them using her tricycle and trailer. Now that she knew what rent she was to pay for The Belfry, she was confident of being able to afford a small van.

That was on her to-do list.

At one o'clock, she returned to The Belfry and picked up her besom. It was a gift from James, and she had a notion she might be needing it. She set off at a brisk pace into Fiddle Bay.

Mitch was parked at the post office, and she greeted him with a kiss. "All right then. How do we get to your mum's place? Through the cove gateway where the bats went?"

Mitch shook his head. "No, my love. Ayesha can't be doing with seawater."

"How, then?"

"We'll drive down to Sydney and go through the castle bridge gate, and then to Mum and Dad's place."

"They live *over there*."

"Mostly."

She'd thought so. This was going to be an adventure. First time *over there*, to the place she thought of as Fairyland. First time meeting Mitch and James' parents. First time meeting Ayesha . . .

"Let's go," she said.

Chapter Six: Over There

The castle bridge gateway turned out to be near Glebe. Mitch pulled into a parking space near a row of terrace houses and led the way to a courtyard in one of the fenced gardens.

"I'd love to introduce you to the bridge keeper, Mistress Joan, but today we don't have time," he said. He took her hand. "You haven't been *over there* before?"

"No. I'm new to all this."

"Then there are a few things you need to know. We'll have to hold hands as we *go,* to make sure we end up in the same place."

"What if—"

"I won't lose you. I promise. When we get to where Mum and Dad live, then you can move normally, but I think it would be best if we stay hand in hand, so Ayesha sees the state of play immediately."

"Right." She tugged at his hand. "I'll try to look like a cat-loving-person—"

"Don't try to look like anything, my love. Just be as you are."

She nodded.

Mitch squeezed her hand. With his free hand, he reached for a low gate and flicked the latch. As far as Queenie could see, it led to another part of the courtyard. Beyond it, she saw a tomato cloche and a hedge.

Mitch opened the gate and took two steps through, bringing Queenie with him.

Then he paused, to let her take in her surroundings.

"Wow!"

She gazed around in wonder. They had emerged under a stone arched bridge. Around them grew a dense thicket of some plant with creamy foaming flowers or seed-heads. Queenie couldn't be sure which. Away to one side, the ground sloped up to an actual castle.

Of course. Castle bridge gate.

"Shall we?" Mitch murmured.

"Oh, yes."

Queenie held on to his hand with a death grip and clutched her besom in the other hand.

"This might look odd to you, but it's fine. You're safe. Close your eyes if you want," he said. He started walking.

For a few paces, Queenie saw the bridge, the plants and the castle . . . a maze and herb gardens . . . trees . . . and then the scene began to blur around her.

It felt weird, as if she'd stepped into fantasy.

Why? What?

She no longer felt the ground, and there was no sensation of speed. It wasn't hot or cold, windy or still.

Are we in a time warp? A wormhole? Hyperspace?

She tried to ask Mitch, but her tongue wouldn't frame the sounds.

Noo wonder yon moggy doesnae want to gang this wa' twice a year!

The only things that felt real were Mitch's hand and the besom. Queenie concentrated on these.

She was glad she'd done that when Mitch slowed. The world returned around her, and she felt grass tickling her ankles.

The warm smell of herbs, currant bushes, hay, and animals bathed her senses, and was that a skylark trilling almost too high to hear?

Mitch stopped, and Queenie felt the ground lurch under her feet. She jammed the besom into the earth to steady herself, jerked to a stop, and tried to regain her balance, dropping Mitch's hand in the process.

"Och, auld Scratch fly away wi' ye!" Queenie exclaimed, and she sat down, hard.

Laughter alerted her to the presence of someone who wasn't Mitch.

Queenie looked up from her undignified position to see a tall, buxom woman standing not far away. She wore a full calf-length skirt in muted plaid, a blue blouse and a wool shawl crossed over her chest. Her hair was mahogany with a liberal streaking of grey, and she had clear grey eyes and a fair complexion. She had a bucket of milk in one hand and a bundle of straw under the other arm.

Queenie perceived she was beautiful in a motherly fashion.

The woman, who looked so much like James that she must be Danna Kingsolver, stopped laughing, although her eyes still shone with merriment. She put down the bucket and said to Mitch, "Mitchell, had ye no better help yon lassie up?"

Queenie shook her head. "I can manage." She used the besom to get upright. Then she approached the woman, holding out her hand.

"Greet you, Mistress Kingsolver." She glanced at Mitch, hoping this was correct.

Mitch's mother tossed the straw bundle into the air. It vanished. So did the bucket of milk. She took Queenie's hand in both hers, and she looked her in the eyes.

"Hello, Queenie Hart."

"I'm sorry I fell over. I'm not usually so clumsy."

"Are ye no'?" Danna Kingsolver's eyes twinkled. "My Jamie said ye'd taken a wee tumble down some stairs and needed mending with some of my salve. I fear the laddie used that to his advantage."

"I did, and he did, but in my defence, there *was* a thunderstorm at the time, and I thought the roof might fall in."

"Quite understandable, then. I should not have laughed . . . but oh, the look on your face!" Danna spoke in a softer version of James' accent.

She let go of Queenie's hand and turned to Mitch, extending her arms for a hug. "Greet you, my dear son. It's grand to have ye back."

"It's good to *be* back," Mitch said. He cleared his throat. "Mum, Queenie and . . . and James . . . and I—"

"Aye?" Danna looked surprised.

Mitch stalled.

Of course! Until a few days ago, Mitch had always avoided mentioning his other self, so of course his mother was taken aback.

Queenie said, at random, "Thank you for the currants, mistress."

"It was a pleasure, dearie. The crop was extra fine last year."

"And thank you *so* much for this." Queenie fished the thistle pendant out of her blouse. "Jamie gave it to me, and I wore it to the Halloween Ball. Mitch says you want me to have it . . . but I'm not sure. It's an heirloom, isn't it?"

It must be worth a great deal, too, but Queenie didn't think it polite to mention that.

"Aye, it was a gift to my granny from her man's maniman," Danna said. "And verra surprised she was, so I hear, being seventy at the time. Having the Pict hand her such a thing fair flummoxed her." She cocked her head. "But maybe you dinnae know of the Pict?"

"I do, actually. Jamie told me a bit about him."

James had said his great-grandfather's manifestation self was a howling blue savage with a high devotion to woad, who smelled of wet fleece, but that sounded a bit bizarre when associated with a piece of floral jewellery, even to Queenie.

"Aye, a sight to behold. That mannie was . . . let's say he wasnae shy. He liked to ravish my granny in the heather." She chuckled. "Mind, Granny Jean was up for it, which was as well."

Queenie was used to the frankness exhibited by the fay, unless, like Mitch, they were trying to hide something, so she just smiled.

"The thistle gaud came to me when I had enough years. I was the only granddaughter, see. I wore it now and again. I was minded to wear it when I wed Beaman, but he gifted me a wedding necklace he'd crafted, and how could I say no to *this*?"

She untied her shawl to reveal a fine gold chain strung with gold bees.

"That's lovely," Queenie said.

"Aye, I think so. I've never taken it off since the day he hung it around my neck. That said, the thistle gaud is no' suitable for tending goats and hens, ye ken? And I could not give it to any of my misses or theirs — no pixie miss would want to wear it." She added comfortably, "It becomes ye well and I know you're the perfect lassie to have it."

"How? You don't know me . . ."

"No, dearie, but my boys do — my lad and my laddie. I love them both dearly, but I never could make them civil regarding one another. One spoke resentfully of his brother. The other would not speak of *his* brother at all. I hoped one day someone would do it — a lassie strong enough to mend the rift. I'm that glad ye've come to us. I was starting to fear I'd be off to glory before I saw them wed and settled."

Wed? Queenie's mind stuttered at the concept, although she was unsure why.

I cannae wed twa men . . . not that either has asked me.

41

Mitch came and put his arm around her. "You've a good few years yet, Mum," he said to Danna.

"Aye, so I have, and maybe more than I feared now I can stop worrying about the pair o' you. I *can* stop, Mitchell?"

Mitch nodded. "James and Queenie have arranged things between them so he and she will live together during October."

"And you, my son?"

"I want to live with her too."

"Is that what *you* want, Queenie?" Danna asked.

"I do, but there's one wee impediment."

"Aye?"

"Ayesha," Mitch said. "How has she been?"

Danna held out her hand and waggled it. "Middling," she said.

"Better than usual, then?"

"Aye, until a few days past when she took it into her heid to hie her to the gateway. Mistress Joan sent her back wi' Trollie, clawing and spitting."

"Ouch," Mitch said.

Danna laughed. "No harm. Claw though she might, she'd make no impression on that auld mannie's hide. Trollie thought it a good joke."

"I'm sorry it came to that though," Mitch said. "I should have fetched her home as soon as I was back."

"You should, but I see why you didna. Couldn't tear yourself away from the lassie's bed." She shrugged. "Can't blame you for that, lad. What do ye plan to do about yon moggy?"

"We're working on that. I may be a fix it pixie, but as you know . . ."

"Fixing your own affairs is often beyond you," his mother said. "I could keep her by me, if it will help."

"I know you would, but I think that must be a last resort," Mitch said. "James really can't look after her, so in October we

42

do need you, but I don't expect you to fix my mess."

Danna said, "I don't pretend I'm longing to have Mistress Spit-Spat with me all the time, especially right now. She's in a mood."

"Mitch brought me to meet her, so we can see what she thinks of me," Queenie said.

"It's an idea," Danna said, nodding. "Come to the house, dearies. I'll put the kettle on."

A short stroll over the hill brought them to the house. It was a long low farmhouse, built of grey stone with white-washed trim. Danna led them through a flourishing garden where flowering plants mixed with fruit and vegetables in a bright confusion, then she went in to make tea.

Mitch took Queenie's hand. "Ayesha will be in the main room. I won't let her harm you."

Queenie drew a deep breath. She had little sympathy for a cat who had been rescued three times over and who attacked poor James. On the other hand, Ayesha evidently believed Mitch was hers to rule and command, and perhaps it would be unkind to dispossess her.

She's a cat . . . a wee moggy.

She had an idea. "Maybe I should go in alone. James said she's usually okay with other people."

Mitch said, "It's up to you, but please be careful. She's fast and she's tricky."

Queenie went through the door he opened for her. The main room was comfortably furnished with armchairs and a large craft table. There was a case of books, a sewing basket, a loom, some knitting, a partly carded fleece, two flutes, a sketchbook, and a half-carved box with the shavings all about it.

Obviously, the senior Kingsolvers found plenty to do in the evenings.

Ayesha sat on the padded windowsill in a patch of sun.

She was a small and beautiful cat with pale grey fur and a

faint stippling of mackerel tabby stripes. Her ears were large, and her tail was long. She glanced indifferently at Queenie.

"Greet you, Ayesha," Queenie said.

She took a few steps forward. Ayesha glanced at her again. She rose to her feet and stretched into a hoop before she cocked an ear and began to wash.

"You're a pretty thing," Queenie said. She realised she'd built the ice queen into a monster in her mind. Mitch's anxious comments hadn't helped.

Ayesha gave her a limpid look from clear green eyes and uttered a chirrup.

Queenie sat down on the window seat.

The cat went on with her toilette.

Queenie thought, and hoped, that if she sat calmly enough and for long enough, the queen would be moved to make some overtures.

The glances her way became more frequent.

Yes, Ayesha was curious.

Then—Mitch poked his nose into the room.

Ayesha looked up sharply. Her ears flickered and her tail twitched.

Mitch came over and held out his hand. "Greet you, my girl."

She rubbed her face against his hand and then turned her head away to focus on Queenie.

Her eyes narrowed. Her whiskers pricked and swivelled.

Mitch sat beside Queenie and put his arm around her.

Ayesha froze. Her eyes turned into slits, and she spat. Her tail went into overdrive. A strange croon came from her throat, rising to a keen.

"Queenie, love, you'd better back off," Mitch said softly.

Queenie got to her feet. She was about to retreat when a sudden burst of outrage swept through her, pinning her in place.

She turned abruptly to face the cat, and Lassie Haggis surged into her voice. "Weel, weel, so *ye're* yon sleekit moggy who thinks she has the right to make other folk miserable," she jeered. "Ye hurt my Jamie, and ye're seekin' to keep Mitch for yoursel'. I ken fine ye've ruled him for years, but that's aboot to stop, ye hear? He's *no* a slave for a wee bitty creature like yoursel'."

The cat spat at her.

"Sssssist!" Queenie gave it back, with interest. She banged the besom on the floor. "Aye, I swore there'd be a reckoning betwixt ye and me, ma fine wee moggy, and this is it." She took another step forward. "Dinnae cower. I'd never harm ye, nor let ye come to harm. I'll hae ye live wi' me as a grand companion. I'll make fish tarts in yer honour. I'll gie ye all the comforts a wee cat needs. But get this into those big ears Ayesha — ye're going to be civil from now on, or I'll know the reason why." She turned and beckoned imperiously to Mitch.

He came to stand beside her, biting his lip. Queenie thought he was stifling laughter.

She twined one arm around his neck, and she snuggled in and kissed him with intent. "Mine," she told the cat, over her shoulder. "Mine to love and to bed wi'. Yours to honour and to love if love ye even can." She put down the besom and picked up the ice queen. "Nae more spitting and nae more foolish sulks! Ye hear?" She handed her to Mitch.

Ayesha hung limply from Mitch's hands. Her ears swivelled and her eyes skittered. She looked about to leap and run.

Then, gradually, she relaxed. She settled into Mitch's arms and looked up at him with a questioning chirrup.

"Yes, my lady, you're coming home with me," Mitch said gently. "I'm sorry I was gone so long, but it can't be helped."

"Home wi' *us,* and it dinnae need to be helped," Queenie corrected. She kissed Mitch again, seeing Ayesha's ears flatten. "I said, *nae more,* moggy. Now, come here to me."

She took the unresisting cat from Mitch and sat down on the window seat again, holding Ayesha in her lap.

She stroked her, feeling the defensive muscles relaxing into calm. Ayesha was a beautiful creature.

Danna came in with a tray of tea.

Her brows rose a little at the sight of Queenie with the grey terror relaxed in her lap, but she nodded with approval.

"Ye've a good hand with animals, Queenie."

"I'm a dog person, really," Queenie said. "We're going to get one."

"We are?" Mitch sounded confused.

"Yes. You like dogs and so do I. James is verra fond of them. Therefore, we're getting a dog, and Ayesha is going to get along with it."

She accepted a cup of tea from Danna.

Chapter Seven: The Second Tart

Queenie Hart, November 5th, 2021

Ayesha seemed understandably confused when Mitch drove from the post office in Fiddle Bay to The Belfry instead of going back to the *pied-a-terre*.

She was even more bothered when Queenie let them all in.

"Are you really going to make fish tarts for her?" Mitch asked.

"Yes, why not? Salmon with capers, I think, with a very thin, crisp shell. That way she can eat the filling without making a mess."

"That sounds tasty. Will Oliver like it?"

"Possibly not, but he forgot to specify *sweet* tarts for his Christmas bounty. I will make most of them sweet. I wonder how mandarin segments would work with salmon—no, lemon!"

Mitch said, "Wafer-thin slices of lemon."

"Perfect—though I will leave that out of Ayesha's share. And I might try a white fish variation for her too."

Queenie took the unresisting cat from his arms and tickled her under the chin. "All right, my lady, I'm going to put you down. You can choose a place to sleep. It will be all your own."

She put the cat down.

They watched her wander around the main room, sniffing delicately at chairs and table legs.

Does she detect James' presence?

"Has she a bed at your place?" Queenie asked.

"Yes . . . a wicker basket with a blanket."

"When she's chosen a place, maybe you could get it for her."

"I will."

The cat continued her explorations.

"She'd probably like the belltower, but she wouldn't enjoy the bats," Mitch said.

Queenie said, "She could have it most of the year, and since she's going to your mum in late September, the bats won't be an issue."

"It could work," Mitch said.

Queenie frowned. "Where's she gone?"

He shrugged. "She's a phaser."

"Yes, so James said — but what *is* that, exactly?"

"She walks through doors."

"So do I," Queenie pointed out.

"When they're closed."

"Oh."

"Walls too, and I suspect she can also dissolve through wooden floors, although I've not seen her do it."

They found Ayesha in the belltower, perched on a stool with a cushioned top.

Queenie had spotted it there before, but she hadn't bothered to investigate. Now she did so, by plucking Ayesha off the stool.

The top lifted off, revealing a hollow lined with a few old volumes of sheet music.

A piano stool . . . no, an organ stool. I wonder where the organ is?

"How about this for her bed?" Queenie asked.

Mitch double-tapped his wrist, and a soft blanket appeared. It looked hauntingly familiar, made in shades of blue, grey and green.

"Is that James' blanket from his basket of childhood?"

Queenie asked.

"No, it's mine. Mum gave it to me, and I gave it to Ayesha."

"As tribute?"

"No, my own love. I gave it to her because it's made of braeside wool and is pretty well indestructible. I can clean it with a shake."

"Your mother is brilliant."

"She is. She makes practical things beautiful . . . and vice versa."

"She's exactly the right mother for you and for James."

He glanced at her sideways. "And yet, she couldn't get me to acknowledge James. And before you fly at me, I'll point out that *he* was none too complimentary about me."

"Verra true."

Until Queenie brought him to order, James had been inclined to speak of his other self as *he,* in no fond terms.

Mitch went on, "It took *you,* my own dear love, to bring about that alchemy. For that, Mum will love and honour you forever."

"It was my wish," she said.

"Oh?"

"You know full well James gave me a wish. I wished that he could be lucky and loved . . . the only way for that to happen was for *you* to allow it, and so, my darling Fixer, it has come to pass."

Mitch tucked the blanket into the hollow of the seat.

Queenie put Ayesha on the floor. She leaped up and began kneading the blanket into shape.

Mitch put his arms around Queenie, bent his head and rested his forehead against hers. "I love you into forever and beyond."

"I love you." She snuggled against him.

He said, "That love is tinged with regret. I feel selfish in having such a gift as you. James has so little."

"That's not the way to look at it. I promised him a fair and equal share of love and attention."

"One twelfth," Mitch said.

"No. One lifetime. Just the same as yours."

"I suppose . . ."

"It's the only way to look at it."

"You'd better tell him."

"He knows, I expect."

"Show him now."

Queenie stood back out of his arms. He looked at her steadily, his hazel eyes glimmering with what looked suspiciously like tears.

"I will then," she said. She closed her eyes and reached out. "Jamie, my ain dear laddie . . . come close to me."

She put her arms around the man before her, drew in, and raised her face.

She found his lips and kissed him. The scent of eucalyptus dissipated. She smelled clean wool.

A faint vibration reached her ears, reminiscent of the way the bells had disturbed her at Halloween. She decided to ignore it. The bats were gone. It must be a memory.

"Och, Jamie — I loe ye forever."

And I love you, dearie.

The words came into her head in James' broad Glaswegian accent, but when she had kissed him again and opened her eyes, it was her pixie man standing before her.

She gave him a watery smile and moved in for another kiss. "Love you, my Fixer."

Mitch turned her gently to look at Ayesha, who had completed her nest in the music stool.

Queenie puffed out her cheeks. "Is she fixed?"

"I think she's *considering* being fixed," Mitch said cautiously. "She should like this place. She can prowl in the graveyard."

"Good." Queenie threw off melancholy. "The belltower

suits her, I think. She can come here when she wants some peace. Can we shut the door? I don't think Oliver wants random visitors wandering into the belltower, and that might happen if we leave it open."

"Certainly we can shut the door. She'll still come and go."

"Grand." Queenie reached forward and gave her newest housemate a gentle rub behind her ears. "Welcome home, Ayesha."

Ayesha gave her a contemplative look. She didn't purr, but she didn't spit, either.

Queenie hoped they might learn to get along.

She followed Mitch down the spiral and back into the main room. She wanted quite badly to take him to bed. But—"You have a train to meet."

Mitch caught his breath. "So I do. I need to bring my caps here so I can keep track."

"We'll put up some pegs for them," Queenie said.

Mitch kissed her. "I wish I could stay."

"So do I, but you have passengers and I have a fish tart to create."

"So you do. What are you going to call it?"

"The Ayesha, I think," Queenie said.

She watched wistfully as Mitch headed for the door.

"It's Guy Fawkes Day," she said aloud. "And we've nearly made it through without explosions."

Chapter Eight: The Third Tart

Queenie Hart, November 8th, 2021

Three days after Ayesha's arrival at The Belfry, Queenie remembered the birthday gift her parents had sent to her old address in Sydney.

She supposed she ought to retrieve it, but she was reluctant to confront her ex-landlady, Angel Petty.

They had never got along, and their parting had been acrimonious.

Maybe she's let my unit, and the new tenant is keeping mail for me, she thought without much hope.

Mitch was out on Fixer business. He hadn't told Queenie where he was going, or why. It wasn't her concern. She didn't need to check that he wasn't going to go to bed with someone to fix his or her problem, because he'd decided, independently, not to do that ever again.

Jamie will be that relieved.

James had *hated* the one time Mitch did that. It had turned out well, but to James, being a trapped and unwilling witness to a widow's misery had been an agonising burden.

Queenie thought about telephoning Angel Petty, but what would be the point? If the woman had the package, then Queenie would still have to go to Sydney to collect it. She didn't think her ex-landlady would be willing to put it in the post.

Mum was right. I should have told her and Dad I'd moved.

But . . . since when do they ever send me parcels, or even postcards?

Shane and Liberty lived in a mobile home with little room for unnecessary items. Thus they had informed Queenie that the only gift they needed from her for the foreseeable future was her happiness . . . and a phone call now and again to reconnect.

The subtext was that they would provide the same for her, and so they did.

Besides — they'd already given her four considerable gifts. They'd given her life, a brilliantly happy childhood, the knowledge and mental strength to manage her affairs, and a nest egg to use as a house deposit when the time was right.

It wasn't their fault that interest rates had flatlined while property prices soared.

There were two more parental gifts in the equation — one given without conscious decision, and one withheld without malice. The first was Queenie's sometimes-troublesome portion of fay blood. That was a gift from Liberty, who had little idea and not much interest in how she came to have it to pass on. The gift withheld was the acknowledgment and understanding of the Caledonian Curse, and the Lassie Haggis persona that came to stay for October because of that fay blood.

They wouldn't accept it. Maybe they couldn't. Liberty made self-help her vocation. She believed willpower and self-knowledge could solve just about any personality glitch or emotional problem. She used her system to maintain cordial relations with her impulsive and often odd mother, Janet, and her kind but silent father. It worked for her.

Shane, despite being married to a woman with fay ancestry, had never got along with his cousin Branok St Ives, who was half-fay and who, consequently, had personal advantages and powers that Shane must always lack.

Queenie wondered, fleetingly, if Shane had even *known* Liberty had fay blood when he married her. Maybe she hadn't told him. After all, it was irrelevant to her. It didn't show, and it had given her no special talents or advantage.

She has better health than most women her age, but that's about it . . .

Would Dad have married her if he'd known?

He certainly did know now, and Queenie would have bet her life that her parents were happy together. They both had creative talents, and they respected one another's achievements.

She grimaced. These reflections weren't getting her any closer to solving her current problem.

If she'd ever befriended her two neighbours, the lady who knitted and the FIFO worker, she might have asked them to intercede.

No, she'd have to bite the bullet and go to Sydney and beard the Petty in her den.

She glanced at her clock. Better go now.

She changed her shoes and packed a small gift box with her shortbread. Tarts would be a bad idea, after the confrontation her jam-and-ant problem had caused with Ms Petty.

Encouraging vermin indeed!

Before she left, she popped up to the belltower to take her leave of Ayesha.

The cat was perched on a rafter above the bells, apparently watching motes of dust dancing in a ray of sunlight.

Queenie looked up at her.

"Greet you, Ayesha. I'm going to Sydney. I'll be back in a few hours," she said.

Ayesha waved her tail gently.

Queenie left. She knew the cat didn't understand much English, but on some level she was convinced she and Ayesha now communicated with one another. At least, Ayesha understood Lassie Haggis and was rightly wary of her.

She'd got into the habit of telling Ayesha when she was going out, and of greeting her when she returned.

She needs to be important, and she's here for The Belfry when I'm not.

Andy had told her The Belfry would claim her, but it was a gentle claiming. She felt that it liked having a busy, creative, thankful occupant.

I wonder if I were to take my besom to Mother Goose Lane, would it work on Ms Petty the way it did on Ayesha.

Better not.

She didn't believe the besom James had given her at Halloween had magical powers. *She* did *not.* The fact remained that when she wielded it, she felt intrepid and invincible, Ayesha showed respect instead of resentment, and things went *right.*

I'll take it.

She seized it from its accustomed place beside the door to the belltower and let herself out before she could change her mind.

It was a fine spring day, and she made good time on her walk into Fiddle Bay.

As she approached the post office, she smiled and exchanged greetings with people she knew — her local acquaintances who were fast becoming friends.

Duncan Dee from the supermarket called a cheery hello, and Queenie waved back.

Round-faced Duncan had been a great support to Queenie during her difficult October, and she was grateful to him.

"Wanting some tripe this week, Queenie?" he called.

Tripe?

"Maybe," she sang out. After all, she'd tried to order sheep's heads, neeps and pig trotters and other robust comestibles while under the influence of the Caledonian Curse.

Was he joking? Or did he genuinely want to accommodate one of his best bulk customers in her penchant for esoteric ingredients?

Whatever did he think of her marching along, clutching a besom?

Queenie made it to the post office just as the green mini-bus pulled in.

She waited for two passengers to disembark, then she mounted the steep steps, and held out her fare.

"Station, please, driver."

Mitch laughed and took the fare. "Sit by me, sweetheart."

"Sweetheart?"

He shrugged. "Darling love?"

Queenie kissed him. "I'm going to Sydney," she said, although he hadn't asked. "I have to see my old landlady about that parcel from Mum and Dad."

"Have you called them back, yet?" Mitch asked, putting Ethel into gear and pulling away from the park.

"No—I want to find out about the parcel first."

"Do you need the Fixer?"

She gave that serious consideration. "I don't think so. I believe this is something I have to do myself."

"I see you've brought the besom."

"Aye. Can you cast a glamour on it for me?"

Mitch checked in the rear-view mirror. A couple of passengers behind them looked confused. One was looking thoughtful.

Queenie turned and gave them a grin and a wave.

She knew Mitch was much more circumspect about conjuring in public than James was, but what were her fellow passengers like, listening in on a private conversation?

"Anything for you, but it might not last long," he said.

"Never mind then. I'll just be a woman carrying a broom. It's not illegal—is it?"

"Not that I know of," Mitch said.

At Borrowdale Junction, he got out of the bus to help one of the older passengers down. Queenie perceived it was a member of the Chess-Nuts, a group of senior citizens who played regular games of chess at the village green. The Chess-

Nuts liked their luxuries, and they'd lately put in an order for a dozen-and-a-half assorted tarts to be delivered to their table at the green twice a week.

This particular Chess-Nut wasn't Kez, the only one whose name Queenie knew for certain. Despite being a rickety octogenarian with arthritis, Kez fancied both Mitch and James. She flirted with them shamelessly.

The one on the bus today was a different proposition. Queenie thought her name was Maryanne ... or Marion. Something like that.

Mitch turned from helping the Chess-Nut to alight and held out his arms to Queenie.

She didn't need help, but she accepted it anyway, dropping a kiss on Mitch's nose as she reached the ground. "I love you ... and I'll probably be back on the five o'clock."

"Ayesha okay?"

"Yes. You might check her, though."

Mitch's attention was called by other passengers wanting to go to Oakengrove, so Queenie headed for the train.

The Chess-Nut, a tall, grey-haired and distinguished-looking woman who might have been a retired school principal, was catching the same train, so Queenie helped her with her wheeled shopping basket.

"*Bedankt*," said Maryanne or Marion as they took seats in an otherwise empty carriage. Her gaze zeroed in on Queenie's bag ... and the besom. "Do I detect tarts?"

"Shortbread. I'm taking some to my ex-landlady."

"Lucky woman. Are you also taking her that besom?"

"Not exactly." Queenie looked at Maryanne or Marion with renewed interest. "How did you know it's a besom?"

"Isn't it?" She had a faint accent ... possibly German. "You had it as part of your costume at the Halloween Ball."

"I did, but most people thought it was a broom."

"Clearly a besom, my *vriend*." Maryanne or Marion gave

Queenie a sudden grin and leaned forwards, bringing with her a waft of phlox. "I'm not sure if we've ever been properly introduced. I'm Madelief van Zijl."

Not Maryanne or Marion.

"If you can't get your tongue around that, you can always call me Maidy."

"Thanks," Queenie said. "I'm—"

"Queenie Maeve Hart. I know."

Queenie frowned.

"You're wondering how I happen to know your middle name . . . I could be mysterious and look knowing, but it's perfectly simple. I'm a friend of Danna Kingsolver, whose sons have been bending her ear about their desire for the very charming Queen of Tarts."

"*Sons.*"

"Ja, sons. Mitchell I knew as a child—James, not so much. To discover the pair of them driving a bus in Fiddle Bay this year was a—surprise. Therefore, I recently went to visit Danna to find out all the gossip."

Queenie tightened her grip on the besom, unsure where this was going. "Mistress van Zijl, are you fay?"

"Mevrouw van Zijl is the way I usually style it, but yes, I am. How clever of you."

"You gave me enough hints," Queenie said.

The woman leaned back. "I wanted to say I'm glad Danna's sons have someone to love. She has been troubled about them—James especially. It takes a lot to trouble Danna."

"I'm glad I met them," Queenie responded. She added, "Mevrouw, what order are you? I hope that's not an offensive question, but I have a lovely set of books called *The Orders of the Fay* that raises a few questions even though it answers others."

"Not offensive, Queenie. Indeed, I could be said to have invited the question. I'm kanaalfee."

"I see. Do the other Chess-Nuts know?"

Mevrouw van Zijl waggled her hand much as Danna had done when asked about Ayesha's frame of mind. "A few do, I suspect. Most of them take me for a Dutchwoman and assume I know all about cheese, tulips, canals and windmills."

"Do ye no'?"

Lassie Haggis had hijacked Queenie for a moment, and Mevrouw van Zijl gave her an amused look.

"Aye, lassie, I do weel . . ." She laughed at Queenie's chagrined expression. "I have several braefolk friends, and many of them are more broadly spoken than Danna," she explained.

The train slowed, and the woman got up, moving much more freely than she had at Borrowdale. "I'll see you later, Queenie. Thanks for the chat. By the way, the Chess-Nuts are having a Christmas party on the twenty-third of this month. These things get earlier and earlier. If I had *my* way I'd ban any mention of Christmas before December. However, I'm breaking my rule to give you the heads-up that we'll need a large order of tarts and that delightful shortbread. Do you happen to make mince pies?"

"I do," Queenie said.

She didn't, but now she would.

"Excellent. I'll get an order form from your website and send it to you in plenty of time."

She stepped out of the carriage, saying, just before the train moved on, "Maybe your ex-landlady is not so lucky if you're taking that besom along."

Queenie rolled her eyes.

Kanaalfee. Weel, weel.

Kanaalfee, she recalled from Volume Three of her set, were not too common. The author, Piers le Fay, with his characteristic lack of definite opinion, mentioned that some experts considered kanaalfee as a variant of the much more numerous alpenfee, some thought they were manifestations of other orders, and still others suspected they were the result of non-specified fay intermarrying with the Dutch prior to the

Industrial Revolution. The kanaalfee themselves claimed not to know either, but they *were* highly knowledgeable about cheese—and tulips.

Queenie pulled out her phone and made a note about mince pies. Maybe it would be possible to make a mince tart for Oliver's Christmas order? She began to look for some historical recipes on her phone.

A surge of excitement struck her as she discovered mince pies were once made from a mixture of meat and fruit and spices . . . a long way from the modern recipe.

Duncan Dee would be the person to consult about the best cut of beef to use, and she would come up with a recipe for the fruit. Whiskey and orange, perhaps. She'd set the fruit to steep well ahead of her first experiment.

Mitch will be drooling. He's bound to ask what I call it . . .

Ah! A Chess-Nut suggested it, so I'll add chestnut puree to the fruit and call it a Chess-Nut Tart.

Chapter Nine: The Parcel

Queenie Hart, November 8th, 2021

Queenie was so absorbed in her plans for the Chess-Nut tart that she almost forgot to get off the train. She remembered in time, exiting just before the doors closed.

She walked to her old locality, not too far from the station.

Mother Goose Lane sounded like a fairy-tale address, but it was anything but. It was short . . . little more than a cul-de-sac, and there wasn't a goose in sight.

Queenie had lived in one of four identical units, all owned by Angel Petty. Ms Petty lived in another of them.

Queenie saw that nothing much had changed since she'd left in a hurry halfway through August.

She took the simplest approach first, walking to her ex-unit and knocking on the door.

After a minute or so, the door opened partway. "Yes?" The voice was crisp and musical, but the woman behind it was sturdy and rounded, with an unbecoming brown bob. She looked doubtfully at Queenie through owl-eyed spectacles, focusing on the besom.

"I'm not buying," she said.

"Weel, I'm no' selling!" Queenie snapped. She closed her eyes for a second and then said, "I beg your pardon. My name is Queenie Hart."

"Am I supposed to know you?"

"Not unless you like tarts."

The new tenant took a step backwards.

"To eat, I mean. The thing is, I used to live here. I moved

out a couple of months ago — almost three — and — "

"There was nothing left in this unit when I came," the woman said, beginning to close the door.

"I know. I checked before I moved. But — "

The door kept closing. Queenie snapped, "Will ye stop it wi' the door, woman! Be civil enough to let me hae' ma say, and I'll be oot of your hair, which doesnae suit ye, by the way."

The woman froze.

Queenie said quickly, "My parents called a few days ago and said they sent a birthday present to me here. That's all. I'd like to have it. It will be directed to me, Queenie Hart, at this address. The senders will be Liberty and Shane Hart. I have my driver's licence here — see?"

She dug it out.

The woman stared at her. Her eyes, a surprisingly deep blue, were clear as if . . .

Is she wearing plain glass specs?

"Well, look at it, woman!"

"I don't need to look at it, Ms Hart. No parcel has been delivered here. If it had been, I would have asked the landlady for your new address."

"Would you?"

"Of course I would." The woman patted her peculiarly neat hair. "That would be the right thing to do. Whether she'd have given it to me is another matter."

Queenie deflated. "I'm sorry," she said humbly. "I assumed — "

"You assumed I was the type of person who would keep something not intended for me, or, more likely, bin it. Well, I'm not. You might find out more if you ask over at Unit One."

"So I might," Queenie said dismally.

The woman gave her a slight tweak of a smile. "I wouldn't either," she said.

Queenie dug in her bag again and lifted out the gift box of

shortbread. "Please — take this as my apology for being so un-necessarily rude," she said.

She handed the box to the woman and backed away.

She might have left it at that had Angel Petty not emerged from her unit.

Queenie hesitated for a moment and then she continued on her way.

Her former landlady did the same, and their paths inter-sected.

Angel Petty stopped abruptly. She was much slighter and shorter than Queenie and confrontingly neat. She always gave the impression of being wound up like a crossbow-string. She peered up at Queenie with cool brown eyes.

"Hello, Ms Petty," Queenie said.

"What do you want?"

Considering the last times they'd met Queenie had thwarted an inspection and Angel Petty had refused to return Queenie's bond, the hostility wasn't unexpected.

Queenie got a better grip on the besom. "Since you ask, has a parcel arrived addressed to me?"

A faint gleam lit the landlady's eyes. "Yes, Ms Hart. A par-cel addressed to you did come — on the twenty-seventh of Oc-tober, to be exact."

"May I have it now, please?"

The gleam became more pronounced. "You may not."

"Ms Petty, it *is* mine. You don't have the right to withhold it."

"I'm not withholding anything. I don't have it."

Weel, who does, ye auld —

Queenie said, "I see. Who does have it?"

The landlady said, "If you'd not . . . flitted . . . and had been responsible enough to leave me with a forwarding address, I would obviously have sent it on. Since you did not, it came under the umbrella of unclaimed mail."

"Thank you for letting me know. Goodbye, Ms Petty."

The capitulation tactic had worked with her father's cousin, Branok St Ives. It also worked with Ms Petty.

"Don't you want to know what I did with it?"

Queenie turned back. "No. As you pointed out, I didn't leave you with a forwarding address. You could quite easily have found me, because my new address is on my Queen of Tarts website, but I assume you didn't bother . . . or just didn't think of it.

"By the way—I didn't flit. You gave me immediate notice. I left the same day. I came to your unit to return the key. It's a pity you weren't in to receive it. You obviously got it, since the unit is re-let. In case there is any confusion, I have time-stamped video evidence of me returning the key."

She continued to hold the woman's gaze until Angel Petty looked away. A dull red stained her cheeks and made unbecoming blotches on her neck.

"Goodbye, Ms Petty. I wish you a good Christmas and a happier new year. I really do."

This time, it wasn't a tactic.

She walked away, feeling calm and grounded.

Questioning Ms Petty further would have been useless. At least this way she had left with her dignity intact.

Not to worry.

She considered going on to Circular Quay, where she had spent Halloween afternoon with James. She could get coffee at the O-Quay Café, or ride the ferries, or head to the fairy gardens or even try to locate Lady Lane and call on the ladies at Fairings.

It would have been fun—possibly, but she felt melancholy. Her gift from her parents was gone. She hadn't expected it, and hadn't needed it, but it must have been special for Liberty to break her own self-imposed rule about gifts. More than that, Circular Quay would remind her of James.

They'd had such a lovely day.

I might go to Glebe and find the terrace house with the gateway.

I could probably ask Mistress Joan to let me through.

And then what? She'd like to see Danna again, but she knew she couldn't *go* as she had with Mitch. She'd be in a very strange land without a map. She'd have to find someone who knew the Kingsolvers and ask for an escort. Mitch had said people *would*, but it seemed an imposition.

She boarded the train home.

The minibus was waiting at Borrowdale Junction.

Mitch's face lit into a smile. "Queenie, love! Did you get your parcel?"

"No—but it doesn't matter. Mitch, did you know Mevrouw van Rijn was friends with your mum?"

"Who?"

"The tall lady—one of the Chess-Nuts. You drove her to the station this morning."

"Oh, you mean Madelief. Yes, I did know, but she's never mentioned it, and so neither do I."

Queenie held out the fare.

Mitch looked at it and shook his head. "You don't need to do that when we're alone. In fact, you really don't need to do that at all."

"I suppose not." She settled beside him. "No one else booked?"

"No, this is the Queenie Hart Express."

Queenie said, "Mitch, what are you going to do about the *pied-a-terre*?"

He gave her a surprised look. "It's paid up until the end of the year, but after that I won't renew. If that's convenient with you?"

"That's verra convenient. I told you I want a mannie in my bed to give me comfort and delight."

Mitch said quietly, "Actually, Queenie, I think you told James that. Sometimes it's difficult for me to untangle the conversations."

She'd suspected that.

"I think you're right . . . but I was talking about you, even if I wasn't talking *to* you."

"You might just as well have been talking about him, though."

"In that case, I wasn't. So, now Ayesha has decided to bow to the inevitable, there's nothing to prevent you from moving in with me permanently."

"Except for October," he said. "Queenie, you're going to have James in your bed then."

"Aye. You know that. He deserves happiness as much as you or I."

"Mum is happy with the idea — well, you heard her."

"She says you won't need to worry about you two anymore."

"I'm glad of that. It was something I never could fix on my own," he said, as they entered Fiddle Bay. "No one at the post office stop. We'll just go to Oakengrove, and if there's no pickup there, we can go home."

Home. She liked the sound of that. Then she remembered something. "Mitch, I need to stop at Fiddle-de-Dee to talk to Duncan about minced beef. Can you drop me off there and do the Oakengrove run? I'll walk home."

He glanced at her.

"Everything's all right," she said gently. "I'm working on Oliver's Christmas tart order. I have a recipe to try, but it takes a deal of preparation . . . steeping and soaking . . . so I won't begin until tomorrow. Meanwhile, I'm in a fix."

"Another one?"

"Aye. I'm gey hot in the coochie, so when I get home, I'd like it fine if there should be a handsome pixie man in our bed . . . stripped and in an *extreme* state of readiness." She paused, and then she added, "That's if the Fixer is willing, naturally."

"The Fixer could not be more willing."

CHAPTER TEN: THE FOURTH TART

Queenie Hart, November 8th, 2021

Queenie arrived at The Belfry carrying a kilo of fine minced beef, a bottle of apricot brandy, and some high-quality dried fruit and a bag of chestnuts.

She hadn't purchased tripe, but Duncan had delayed her a while because he wanted to discuss other speciality foods she might have for Christmas.

She put the beef in the fridge and left the other things on the kitchen bench.

Ethel was parked in her accustomed place, so Queenie was confident her Fixer was in residence.

She walked up the steps to the mezzanine bedroom.

Mitch was lying in bed, apparently staring at the double frame on her nightstand.

"Are you planning to hex that, my darling Fixer?" she asked.

He turned to look at her. "No. I was just . . ." He shrugged.

"It's a lot to come to terms with," she said.

"There's no viable alternative."

She sat on the bed, hoping to lighten the tone. "Would you like me clothed, or not?"

"Not," he said.

"Can you make that happen?"

He seemed nonplussed.

"Can you have my clothes off me?" She tapped her wrist to show him what she meant.

"I can try!"

He looked straight at her, and then he double-tapped his wrist.

"Glory be!" Queenie exclaimed as she was suddenly bare.

Mitch grinned at her. "I *can* do it. I wondered. You see, most of us can't interfere with anyone else's clothing. Mum stopped being able to dress or undress me when I was five or six. But of course, you asked me directly."

She rocked on her toes. "You left my shoes on."

"Safety precaution. I didn't want you to fall over when your aspect ratio changed."

"My — och, never mind." Queenie kicked off her shoes and pulled the quilt back. "Lawks!" She stared at Mitch.

"You *said* in a state of extreme readiness," he pointed out.

"And you are — you *certainly* are! That thing looks as if it might go off at any minute."

He held out his arms. They rolled together, and Queenie welcomed him in.

It was over too soon, but she knew from growing experience that Mitch would soon be up for more.

She said, "You remembered to hold hard?"

"Yes." He kissed her, then slid the familiar cloth into her hand. "Queenie, you said something about babies," he added, as if in logical progression.

"Aye, so I did. Not yet, but maybe sometime. Is that something you would want?"

"I would. But have you thought it through?"

"Not entirely. James likes the idea. He said that if you and I had babies, he'd be *Auncle Jamie* and overindulge them."

"He likes children," Mitch said dryly. "He never had a childhood, so he enjoys helping other people to enjoy theirs."

"So I gathered. I suppose he would be an actual uncle to any children we had. Not a courtesy one, I mean."

"More or less." Mitch started fussing with the pillow.

Clearly, he had something on his mind.

"What is it?" Queenie asked.

He gave her the quick *glance and away* he used to do. She'd since decided that had been when he was fighting himself over whether to tell her his secret.

"Mitch, we agreed to tell one another the important things."

"I know. I will."

"Then do," she said, gently. She shifted up the bed and brought his head over to her breast. "Just say what you need. I promised I'd never reject you again, and I won't."

He sighed. "I love this so much."

With a pang, she remembered James saying almost exactly the same thing, although they'd both been clothed.

Mitch said, "About James—and children. I don't know how many you would want. You're an only child."

"Maybe two," she said.

"Then maybe James—" He broke off.

"Maybe James would like to have his own child with me?"

He nodded against her shoulder.

"We did touch on that, but we didn't come to any decision. Neither of us knew if it would even be possible. *Do* manifestation selves ever have children?"

"The Pict did."

Queenie tried to get her head around that. From what she'd heard of Mitch's great-grandfather's second self, he didn't seem exactly user friendly. To be sure, Danna had said he liked to ravish her Granny Jean in the heather . . . but did she really agree to bed a savage with a love of woad?

"Wh-what happened?" she asked.

"A great deal of howling, I should think. I never met him, but Mum did, and she says he was very loud and very blue and mostly very naked.

"He didn't manifest often, but at least one of the children

of that family was his."

"Did they know which one?"

Mitch chuckled. "*He* did. He was usually just a brief mani, but apparently he *persisted* for a whole month once. He brought a gift for Great-Granny . . . wild berries . . .and took her away with him up into the hills. Once the child was born, which happened in a space of time that made the parentage unarguable, he used to come howling down from the hills and take the bairn off with him . . .hill running with it in his arms. Then he'd bring it back to its mother, kiss them both, and . . ." He shrugged. "Great-Grandad would be there in his stead, getting Great-Granny a cup of tea in their bothy."

"Was that child your grandmother? Grandfather?"

"It might have been Granny Elspeth, or one of her brothers. Great-Granny wouldn't tell Mum. She seemed a bit flummoxed by the whole thing, apparently. She *did* tell Mum she had agreed to it all—enjoyed it, even—not wanting her to think she was descended from coercion. Hm. Maybe it *was* Granny Elspeth who was the child."

Queenie saw her family wasn't the only one with secrets. "James won't come howling down from the heather, though. He says he's the most *ordinary* manifestation person your family knows of."

"If it's ordinary to wear argyle sweaters and excite the Chess-Nuts by driving Ethel in a kilt," Mitch muttered.

Queenie, who had been responsible for James' appearance in the kilt, went on, "If he and I did do it—how would you feel about the child? You'd be around it for most of the year. It might want to wear argyle—or have an accent like James."

"I'd love it, argyle and all," Mitch said without hesitation. "I'd give his child with you as much love and commitment as any child *I* got on you. He would do the same for mine, I'm sure. He would have cared for Ayesha if she'd allowed it."

Queenie winced at the thought of how vociferously

Ayesha had not allowed it. James bore three emphatic scars as a consequence.

"It would be confusing for the children," she said.

"That's easily fixed," Mitch said.

"How?"

"Have any wee ones call James and me by our names . . . Dad Mitch and Dad James. That way they will *know* they are ours and yours and loved by all of us."

Queenie drew him closer, snuggling him against her. "Mitch, that would be perfect. So simple, and so reassuring. However did you come up with it?"

"I'm a Fixer, my love. It's what I do."

"There's something else you do," she said hopefully.

"Yes . . . I eat tarts. A great many tarts."

"You can have tarts *after* you do the other thing."

She felt him move his arm. "Oh, no you don't!"

But it was too late. Three Ruby Tuesday tarts popped into sight on the nightstand.

Mitch crammed one into his mouth and hitched up on the pillow to eat it.

Queenie watched him chew.

"Why are you squirming?" he asked, reaching for another one. He bit off the edge, then he licked the jam, his eyes half-closed with pleasure.

"I *love* watching you eat. It makes me—"

Mitch made his way through the second tart with slow enjoyment, apparently unconcerned that Queenie was propped on her elbow, staring at him.

He rolled her over to kiss her and dropped the third one jam-side-down on her chest. "Oops . . . better fix that."

He licked the sticky patch.

Queenie grabbed the tart from him and crushed it against her stomach. "Fix that, noo, before I—"

Mitch fixed it with grave and loving attention.

Queenie quivered, holding back, but soon the sensations became too much for her and she jerked and squealed until there was no more air in her lungs.

In the sticky and satisfied aftermath, Mitch brought her tea in bed.

Queenie felt limp. "That was the most *intense* experience I ever had," she said. "I thought it would never end. It was also the messiest. I'll have to change the sheets."

He beamed, as if she'd paid him a compliment. "I can fix that, my love. So, you enjoyed it? You certainly made enough noise."

"So did you," she countered. "You usually just sigh, or groan a wee bit, but this time, you yelled fit to scare the bats in the belltower . . . if they hadn't gone away. Glory — what if you scared Ayesha off the beam?"

"Nothing scares Ayesha."

"Except my besom."

"That besom scares *me*."

He took her empty cup and kissed her damp brow. "You look so beautiful, all rosy and tumbled and big-eyed."

"Sweaty and sticky and exhausted," she said.

"Yes . . . entirely and utterly yourself."

She smiled. "It was — alarming. Odd."

"What, that I got to eat the Queen of Tarts?"

She chuckled. "You don't get me that way, Mitchell King-solver."

"I thought I just did," he said smugly.

He lay down beside her. "Queenie, I'm *not* being jealous or — selfish. See? I'm not green." He held up his arm, which remained its usual olive.

"What are you talking about? There's nothing jealous or selfish about enjoying me. I enjoy you at least as much. You're what I've wanted for a long time — someone who loves me and who appreciates me. It doesn't hurt that you're beautiful to look at and inventive in bed."

He started pulling at the pillow.

"Mitch!" she said, sharply. "Stop it with the fidgeting. You only ever do that when you're hiding something. Is there something you want to do with me but are not sure I'll allow? Tell me. I can't imagine anything I would dislike along those lines, but I'd soon tell you if it came to the point."

He stopped. "Nothing like that. I only — wondered if we could keep *eating the Queen of Tarts* . . . that way . . . as something just for us. You and me."

Queenie laughed. "Well, I'm not aboot to allow anyone else to eat me that way!" She wanted to add, *Wheest, mun!* but that would be Lassie Haggis speaking, and Lassie belonged to —

She sat up. "Oh, you wanted to know if I'd do the same thing with Jamie when it's his turn!"

Mitch's smooth olive cheeks went an extraordinary shade of green khaki.

Queenie poked him in the ribs. "Well — the answer's no. I haven't bedded James yet . . . although we *have* slept together . . . but James is a shortbread man. He was out of reason cross that *you* claimed *his* tarts, but he has decided he prefers shortbread, and I don't see that as a viable option in bed, do you? Too many crumbs in uncomfortable places. And before you start feeling bad for him — again — I'll tell you — remind you — that *he* was gloating about getting to *hold the October lassie* through the night . . . something you will never do because of the availability issue. So, honours are even." She poked him again. "Fair and equal rights to my attentions, remember? And that means getting to have certain *private* attentions for you only. I don't know what James will ask for when it's his turn, but he will *not* be eating the Queen of Tarts and making her scream while she ends up with jam in her . . . well. And — oh!"

"What?" Mitch half sat up. The uncomfortable green

colour had gone from his cheeks.

"I've just had an idea for a new tart," Queenie explained.

His eyes took on the greedy look she loved. "Tell me about it. All about it."

"It's going to be called the *Fair and Equal*. It will have a divided filling. One half will have vanilla and caraway, and a few flecks of purple thistle flower to give it a shortbread flavour."

"What about the other half?"

"That's *your* share, so what do you propose?"

She thought he'd ask for the plain Ruby Tuesday filling, but he said, "Is it possible to do something with pistachios?"

Pistachios . . . She visualised the greenish-brownish nuts that could be made into paste.

"Yes. I'd need to add something to make it set, but it would work as a nice contrast." She added, "I never knew you liked pistachios."

"Well . . . vanilla and caraway will give a peely-wally pale freckled *braeman* vibe —"

"Stop right there," Queenie said, laughing. "So you think you should be represented as a green and jealous pixie man."

"One you love," he said, sounding unrepentant.

"One I love."

Chapter Eleven: The Fifth Tart

Queenie Hart, November 15th, 2021

Orders for Christmas tarts had begun to come in. Queenie found it difficult to carry enough tarts to the local market using her tricycle, so she started actively looking for a small van.

Mitch protested that he could easily do deliveries for her, but his business was also picking up, as clients all over the greater Sydney area found themselves in fixes with deliveries needed, time-tight appointments to access, and emergency repairs to be made.

"You know I'll always put you first," he said when she pointed this out.

"Yes, and I will hold you to that, but *only* when necessary." She smiled at him. "You are not going to start tying yourself in knots trying to fix things for me, darling Mitch. I'm capable of sorting my own business . . . almost always."

He agreed, although with obvious reluctance. "Just one thing . . . would you allow a distant relative of mine to source you a van? He's an odd bloke, but what he doesn't know about vehicles isn't knowable."

"By all means, wheel him out," Queenie said cordially.

"Just like that?"

"Just like that. I trust you one hundred percent, and it will save me from possibly buying a lemon."

Mitch looked gratified. "I'll have him come by as soon as he can."

Curiouser and . . .

Mitch went off to fix something and Queenie sorted out orders. She was looking forward to meeting one of Mitch's relatives. So far, she knew Danna—and James—and had met Beaman very briefly at the end of her second visit to the Kingsolver house *over there* a couple of days before.

Beaman must have been well into his sixties, but he looked exactly like an older version of Mitch. Queenie loved him on sight, and he greeted her with a hug and a kiss on the cheek, enveloping her in the rich and complex scent of honey.

"Greet you, my dearest relief," he said. He even sounded like Mitch.

My dearest relief?

Beaman chuckled, indicating the thistle gaud that Queenie was wearing with her favourite grey pinafore and a eucalyptus-green blouse. OTT as it was, it lit up the rather plain outfit.

"I'm glad to have that extraordinary piece in the hands of a maid so well qualified to wear it," he explained.

Queenie knew, from her perusal of her books, that *maid* was a generic term for any female fay. She also knew Beaman would never call her a *miss* because she was neither pixie nor pisky.

She smiled. "Thanks, Master Kingsolver."

"Beaman . . . or *father-by-love*, if you're so moved," he corrected. He cast a sly glance at his wife. "I'm glad to have that thing out of my bonnie lassie's kist. It's been silently reproaching me for decades for not being a twa-in-one. And I hear you have tamed the fell feline that has blighted my sons' lives for too long?"

"I wouldn't say that, exactly," Queenie said. She added, "The necklace Danna wears is lovely. She said you made it."

"I did, and I charmed every bee."

"Aye, so he did, the rogue," Danna said, laughing. "It willnae come off!"

"Why?"

Danna shrugged, patting the delicate necklace affection-ately. "Beaman's a pixie man, and he was doing what pixie men do when they get their hands onto something they want."

Beaman had gone out to tend his hives at that point, carry-ing with him two tarts for what he termed *thoughtful consump-tion.*

Queenie smiled at the memory. James had taken his mother's maiden name as his surname because, he'd told her, although he loved his dad very much, Beaman already had a son in his image.

Now she'd met him, Queenie saw exactly what he'd meant.

To be sure, Beaman seemed more relaxed than Mitch, but he was older. His children were grown, and his wife clearly adored him despite her precise pointing out of his motives.

Queenie wondered what this new relative she was going to meet would be like.

Thinking of Beaman with his scent of honey gave her an idea for another Christmas tart. She'd made honey-sweetened tarts before, but she might make the filling almost entirely of caramelised honey, topped with a marzipan bee. The pastry would need to be crisp.

It would be simple and elegant, and if she added a little almond essence to pick up the marzipan notes . . . Queenie hugged herself. *The Beeman.* She'd spell it that way, but she'd tell Mitch and Beaman himself of its provenance.

Mitch will be so excited.

She smiled. His delight in the Christmas tart project made her love him even more.

She thought of calling Duncan Dee to discuss the best sources of local honey, but why not ask Beaman? She was sure he'd give her some of the honey his bees made *over there.* She'd seen great golden jars of it in Danna's pantry. She could offer him tarts in exchange. She'd ask Mitch to arrange it when he returned.

"Five down, seven to go," she said aloud.

She had been making notes in her phone, but now it was time to make a more formal listing of names, ingredients, sizes and methods.

She said, rolling the names around her mouth with pleasure, "Bats in the Belfry — caramel and chocolate. The Ayesha — salmon with lemon. Chess-Nut Tart — antique mince pie filling, The Fair and Equal — vanilla and caraway and pistachio paste and now, The Beeman — honey and marzipan."

CHAPTER TWELVE: A SHOCK

Queenie Hart, November 15th, 2021

Queenie took photographs of the first four tart samples she had prepared, but then she had to put the twelve tarts of Christmas, as she had begun to think of the project, aside to fill more orders.

She was deep in a batch of Strawberry Fool on the Hill, and rather wishing the fiddly confection wasn't *quite* so popular, when her phone rang.

Queenie went on stirring with one hand while she dragged the phone from her pocket.

"Queen of Tarts—Queenie Hart speaking." She'd picked up that greeting from her friend and junior landlord, Andy Tredennick who used something similar when answering his work number.

"Queenie?"

I just said so —

But she'd done the same thing the first time she'd called Andy.

"Yes?"

Belatedly, she recognised the voice. "Mum! Is anything wrong?"

"No," Liberty Hart said.

"Then why—oh. I promised to call you back, didn't I."

"No, the peculiar young man in your bed said you'd call us back."

Queenie let that pass. Mitch, beloved joint-love-of-her-life, might well be termed peculiar by the uninitiated. But then,

Liberty *wasn't* uninitiated. Not entirely.

"I intended to, but I got side-tracked."

"By—"

"By work, and rent, and—"

"Are you managing all right for rent?"

"Didn't we agree that I was to be emancipated . . . autonomous . . . in charge of my destiny?"

"I know what we agreed." Liberty sounded testy. "But Queenie, interest rates are *abysmal*. Your dad and I truly thought your nest egg would grow."

Queenie gasped and stopped stirring for a few seconds. The strawberry mixture popped bubbles, and she hurriedly took it off the stove.

I forgot my nest egg! Must go and see Branok and Gillan before *Mitch's relative comes up with a van.*

"Mum, I've got to go."

"No!" Liberty snapped.

"Ye ken weel ye've no' the right—*dammit!*" Queenie gasped again and hauled her diction back to Queenie normal. "Sorry, Mum. Yes, I owe you a phone call. Let's start again. Is there something important? Is Dad there?"

"Your dad's out, doing a quote for a job. I wanted a private talk."

"Okay. Go ahead."

Liberty drew an audible breath. If it had been Shane calling, he'd have said, at that point, *You know we love you, right?* Liberty, being Liberty, just said, "Are you happy in your new place?"

"Ecstatically," Queenie said.

"Found a job?"

"Not as such. My tart business has done better than I ever hoped for. If you look up my website, you can see."

"I'm glad you've found your niche. Creativity is key."

Queenie said, gently, "Is it so surprising I'm a creative pastrycook? You and Dad are both creatives. You've made a whole living from your Harts Ease platform, and Dad's far more than your average tradie."

"Yes. Your dad's an odd mixture of *bloke* and *artist*. He always says *what you see it what you get*, but he's more complex than that. I think—Queenie, do you remember Shane's rather odd cousin? Branok St Ives?"

"Yes, of course." Queenie didn't add that Branok and his wife had taken charge of her nest egg for her so she wouldn't accidentally squander it while in the grip of the Caledonian Curse. She also didn't add that it was entirely down to Branok that she was able to rent her beloved Belfry.

"He's memorable, I suppose," Liberty said.

"What about him?"

"Your dad hardly ever mentions him. They don't get on."

"I know." She remembered Branok admitting it was mostly his fault and saying he would like to be on a better footing with his cousin.

"I suspect your dad's duality is somewhat to do with his relationship with Branok, growing up," Liberty pronounced.

"Undoubtedly."

"You've given it some thought?"

"It's obvious, isn't it? Branok is a halfling and a pisky at that. He's . . ." She ran down. How to describe the enigma that was Branok St Ives? Supercilious, conscientious, sharp, kind . . ."He's the way Dad might have been if he'd had fay blood instead of being entirely human," she said.

Liberty was quiet, possibly startled. "I think . . . you hit the nail on the head. Shane was the elder, bigger, possibly stronger . . ."

Queenie sincerely doubted that.

"And yet Branok surpassed him without even trying."

She doubted that, too.

"I think Shane probably became a high achiever in his field . . . and adopted the blokey persona . . . to compensate."

"Very likely. Mum, while we're on the subject of fay blood, do you *really* not know which of your relatives was the fairy in the bed?"

"Well, that's straight to the point," Liberty said.

"I need to be."

"I really don't know. An old woman—Mum called her Auntie Violet—told her she had fairy blood, and she told me. There were no details to be had."

"I have a few clues."

"Does it matter?" Liberty sounded impatient.

"Very much—to me. Because that's what the Caledonian Curse is down to. No, hear me out. I know you don't want to hear this, but it's real and it's in me. I'm stuck with it. And—although I've always hated what it did to my life . . . and especially what it did to my relationship with you and Dad . . . now I understand better I wouldn't be without it for worlds."

"I see," Liberty said in such a dry voice that Queenie knew she didn't.

"The Curse isn't a curse. It's something called a manifestation. It comes directly from our fay blood, and what it means is that our hidden ancestor was braefolk. Can you remember anyone—even from a photo—who looked or seemed Scottish? If it was a braewoman, she would have had big hips and a big bosom, and probably a lot of hair. If it was a braeman, he would have been verra tall and broad . . . he might have been a redhead . . . and his eyes, if they weren't glamoured, would have shown heathering."

"What's that?"

Queenie thought of the glorious sight of James' eyes when he was moved by strong emotion. "It's a kind of opalised effect . . . or maybe Northern Lights. Lots of cool colours, purple and grey, teal, silver . . . they shine and cycle. Oh, and whoever it was would have probably had a last name that sounded Scottish."

Liberty said, in a soft, incredulous voice, "Adelaide Southey. My grandmother. One of her brothers, Great-Uncle Don, had strange eyes. There's a photo of him somewhere. And—" She broke off. Then, before Queenie could query her, she said in a rush, "It's nothing these days, of course, but someone told Mum *You're a by-blow.* She had no idea what that meant, and she repeated it to someone. She never found out more, but Mum remembers someone saying *the man isn't around much . . .* or maybe it was *often* or *anymore.*"

"I'll ask her," Queenie said.

"There's no point," Liberty said. "She won't tell you. Apart from that one time, she's never admitted *anything* untoward to me. In fact when I asked her again she said I must have misheard. *I* know what I heard . . . but now she's moved to that retreat—"

Liberty's mother was always trying new things, and Queenie knew from experience she was difficult to find when she went *off on a tangent,* as Liberty put it.

"I see. Thanks, Mum. I don't suppose we'll ever find out exactly what went down. Just one more thing . . ."

"Yes?" Liberty sounded wary.

"Do you *truly* have no fay markers? I mean—"

"I know what you mean," Liberty snapped. "The answer is no. I truly don't. Do you think your dad would have come anywhere near me if I did?"

"Probably not."

And I'm sure you make damned sure you never show them, even if they exist.

There was no point in fighting with Liberty, so Queenie shifted the subject. "I really am sorry I didn't call. Busy, as I said."

"Yes. You always were independent. Your—friend. Is it serious?"

"His name is Mitchell Kingsolver. Mitchell James Stuart Kingsolver. He trades as The Fixer. He also does deliveries for the local supermarket and drives the private shuttle bus between the junction and Oakengrove."

"Oh."

"And it's serious." She felt a smile dawning. "It's more serious . . . and more fun . . . than you can possibly imagine."

"So—he's living with you?"

"Yes. So's his cat."

Liberty said, "Aren't you a dog person?"

"Yes. So's Mitch. He took Ayesha on a few years ago, and he feels responsible for her welfare and happiness."

"I'm glad to hear it. We can never be responsible for another human's happiness, but with animals we have to make that effort."

"Mitch does. And believe me, it's quite an effort."

Liberty went on, "Your dad and I would like to meet him . . . if you don't mind."

"That would be great," Queenie said, secure in the knowledge her parents were thousands of kilometres away.

"Would Thursday the eighteenth suit you?"

"Thursday."

"Yes. Today's Monday. We're in Queensland at present, and we're heading down to Sydney for a conference. We can call in on you on the way. Say, around one o'clock?"

"Fine," Queenie managed.

"That way, we can drop your present off."

"You posted that."

"We did. It came back *not known at this address*. Most irresponsible. Obviously, you left a forwarding address with your landlady."

"Obviously . . ." Queenie said faintly.

"Ah, your dad's coming. Talk later." Liberty blew a kiss down the phone, and the line went dead.

Queenie poked at the congealing strawberry mixture.

And then she finished her sentence " . . . not."

Chapter Thirteen: The Sixth, Seventh and Eighth Tarts

Queenie Hart, November 16th, 2021

Mitch's distant relative turned up on Tuesday morning. Mitch had already left for another Fixer job. Queenie had filled him in on the scant information she'd got from Liberty, included the bombshell of the imminent parental arrival.

He'd professed himself pleased to have the chance to meet Shane and Liberty in the flesh.

"I can take them for a pint. Or a coffee. Or—"

"Yes, do that," Queenie said cordially. On the face of it, letting her pure fay lover loose on her parents was a bad idea, but she had every confidence that Mitch would have things in hand.

She remembered, belatedly, that she hadn't told them Mitch was a pixie.

It was too late now.

Mitch kissed her lingeringly. "If you need anything, call."

"I will," she said.

She was packaging shortbread, Cathedral Window tarts and Irish Shamrocks for a pre-Christmas order when someone knocked on The Belfry door.

It was an abrupt, no-nonsense knock.

Queenie cursed softly in Gaelic and headed for the door. She opened it and came face to face with a teenaged boy standing on the top step.

"Yes?" she said. "Have you come for tarts?"

The boy's bright green eyes swivelled downwards, not to her cleavage, but to the half-filled box of tarts. "I didn't, but I will," he said.

He had a tenor voice and an abrupt way of speaking. He didn't smile. He wore overalls and a green shirt, rolled up to display powerful arms. His hair was ink-black, and his skin so olive it would have made Mitch look pale.

He said, "Are you Queenie Hart?"

"Yes." She looked about for a bike or even a battered ute. He was dressed as a tradie, and he might be old enough to drive—just.

"Peck Grene," he said, offering his hand. It was square and capable, with short, clean nails.

Queenie accepted it.

The boy lifted his left hand and turned it to present the back to her. He waggled his fourth finger.

A wedding ring?

The heavy gold ring gleamed with a deep, contented shine.

The boy contemplated it with satisfaction, then he said, "I have a wife. Chloe. She's—she's *perfect*. She loves me. *Me!*"

"I see," Queenie said faintly. She added, "I expect you're fay?" The question was academic. He was so obviously fay . . . much more obviously than anyone else she'd met.

No human had eyes that colour.

"Pixie man," he said. "Peck Grene."

"So you said."

"Grandad Peter P wanted Peckerdale in my name. Grandad Peter G wanted the Grene. Mum and Dad gave in. No idea why. Mind, my sister's called *Promise*."

"Nice," Queenie said.

Unexpectedly, he laughed. His eyes, which had been challenging and rather scary, softened. "Sorry, Chloe's trying to train me out of doing that. Telling people I'm a married pixie man, I mean. I just can't seem to stop. So happy, you see. Still can't fathom how she can—" He blinked. "I'm a lot older than I look. Thirty-two. I'm a mechanic. I run a repair business down near Patterdale in Victoria. I'm a fix-it pixie."

"Oh," she said, enlightened. "So's Mitch. My lover."

The young man said, "I know. Runs in the family. Great-Granddad Gard Tillien was one. I'm related to Beaman . . . Mitchell's dad, somewhere along the line. Take a leppy gossoon to sort out how. Still, blood and water . . . Mitchell told me you were looking for a van to use for tart deliveries."

"Yes, I am. I need something—"

"Medium sized, reliable, used but not abused, reasonably priced, mechanically sound, comfortable, adaptable, and possibly convertible," he said.

"Yes. That. I don't want to buy a lemon."

"That could be a problem," he said, scowling. "The one I picked out for you *is* a lemon . . . figuratively speaking. A Citroën. Citrus. Get it?"

"I do."

"And it's lemon . . . well, maybe nearer cream. Chloe said lemon cream would just about cover it."

"I expect she's right."

"Chloe is *always* right," Chloe's husband said. "Even when she isn't, she apologises and fixes it . . . and that makes it right, see?"

Queenie stared at the extraordinary young man. "Tart?" She extended the box.

He grinned and took one. "Yum! I need to take some of these home for Chloe. Do you have any that are good for carrying ladies? Because Chloe is having a baby. *My* baby."

"Obviously, your baby," Queenie murmured.

He flashed her another delightful grin. "Not an accident, either. We made it on purpose. I'm so happy I could—"

Tears seeped into his eyes.

"Och, puir wee mannie, hae' ye a kerchief?"

He waved his hand and grabbed one out of the air.

"So that's what it sounds like," he said, mopping his cheeks. "Mitchell said you had a mani." He composed himself and made the handkerchief vanish before continuing. "You know, there's a braeside laddie—a huge, big bugger—lives in the tower where Chloe and I live. He's got a wife he shares with a courtfolk man, and they all run a dance studio. Your mani sounds like *him,* only squared. Cubed." He added, "Hamish Almaclair, he's called. Scared of me. Dunno why." The grin came out again, and Queenie thought the young man knew perfectly well *why.*

He wasn't scary, precisely, but he was unnerving. She wondered if his wife was human, and if so, however she had come to meet *this* specimen, let alone agree to marry him and have his baby. She perceived he smelled of freshly cut grass. Maybe that had something to do with it.

"Okay. I'll give the tarts some thought. Raspberry tea and ginger are meant to be good for pregnant ladies, so I might make something with that."

His eyes widened. "You make tarts *especially*?"

"Aye, I do." She told him about the twelve tarts of Christmas. "I'll order a dozen Chloe tarts then," he said. "Now I expect you want to look at the lemon."

"Yes . . . um, where is it?"

"Back at the garage," he said.

"What—in Victoria?"

"Yes. Couldn't bring it through that godawful cove gateway. For one thing, it wouldn't go *over there.* Cars don't. No one knows why."

Queenie knew that. Piers le Fay, typically, had given a few possibilities.

"I don't know when I'll be able to get down to see it," she said, deflated.

"Oh, you don't need to. I can bring it here, now I can get a fix. Is here okay?" He indicated the turning circle where Mitch usually parked Ethel.

Queenie nodded.

"Okay. Stay there." He retreated down the steps and faced the circle. He lifted his hand.

A pale lemon van popped into sight.

Peck Grene walked up to it and ran his hands over the bonnet as if soothing a horse. "There, lovely thing . . . okay?"

He patted the door. "What do you think?"

Queenie made her way cautiously down to examine the van.

"Take her for a spin." Peck Grene handed her the keys. "I'll have a look round the graveyard. I like graveyards."

"So do I. There's a little spot with three vicars in it. Vicarville, I call it. Go and tell them how happy you are."

"Brilliant idea."

He sauntered off.

Queenie got into the van.

She drove it down to Fiddle Bay and then out to Borrowdale Junction. It answered sweetly to the helm. Everything was in perfect condition.

It felt — right.

She returned to The Belfry determined that this was going to be her van, if she had to — well, whatever she had to do to get it.

"What do you think?" The pixie man was leaning against the belltower.

"I love it. Did you visit the vicars?"

He nodded. "Soothing. I think they were glad for me. Did you know they were fay?"

Queenie stared at him. "I did not."

"Purcell was an elf, Kirk was brae, and I expect Bunting was a hob . . . plain as the nose on your face. Nice nose, by the way."

"So's yours," Queenie responded.

He flashed his teeth, which were big, white and shining. "Chloe thinks so." He evidently contemplated a world where his wife thought his nose was nice, then he switched to business. "I expect you'll want a logo for the van . . . and maybe some artwork? If so, get this bloke . . ." He conjured a pad and scribbled some words and numbers. "This is Kris Peckerdale — my uncle. Bit of a quiet one, but he'll cut you a good deal. He's the best — got an art gallery and all. Kay?"

"Okay." Queenie took the paper. "Um — how much for the van? I can't pay today, but I can — "

He went off in his head somewhere. "Pay anytime. Mitchell said you were good for it. I picked this up for a song and fixed it up. How about we call it fifteen hundred and a few batches of those Chloe tarts? And when our baby is born, you can make a tart in her honour." His eyes went dreamy. "We're going to call her Celadon. Isn't that perfect?"

Celadon Grene.

Queenie said, "Is her second name going to be Jade?"

"No. Fraser. That was Chloe's name before she wed me."

Either he was tired of the joke, or he didn't get it. Queenie felt mean for making it.

He patted the vehicle again.

"I'm off now. Got to see Chloe. Get Mitchell to give me a call when the Chloe tarts are ready. Or you can, of course." He added, "Are you going to wed Mitchell?"

"I don't — we haven't talked about it."

"Do it. It's the best thing *ever*. You get to feel all explody with love and safe at the same time, because she picked *you* . . . or *he* did, in your case. Of course, you'll need to consider the laddie . . . You *do* know about him?"

Queenie nodded, mesmerised.

"Wed him too, then. Only fair. Never met him, but he'll be a good man. Braeman, see. Easier than us pixie men. Faithful. Flori . . . the wife Hamish and Gervais share . . . she wed both of them *and* McTavish and Sir Summer too. So that's four men she's got. Only not all at once. Two at a time. Keeps her busy." He shook his head. "Dunno how she manages it, but she always *looks* happy. So do they."

He lifted his hand abruptly and set off walking.

"Master Grene, do you want a lift to the cove?" Queenie called.

"No thanks, Queenie. I like walking . . . let me know if you ever have trouble with your lemon, but I'm guessing you won't. Just give me a bell when you want it serviced."

"Wait . . . I'll get you some tarts."

"I'll have the box in your hands, if that's okay."

"Go ahead." She remembered her early dealings with her men and said, "I give you permission to conjure this box of tarts."

"Good."

He raised a hand and was suddenly holding the box.

He walked under the dark trees and around the curve of the wall and out of sight.

Queenie had the surreal *what just happened* feeling, but the van was unmistakeably solid, and there. She realised with a small shock that she hadn't signed any paperwork. Was that price solid? Was it enough?

She'd noticed Mitch had problems setting prices, but whether that was to do with his tech-ineptitude or because charging for his services clashed with his fix-it manifestation, she didn't know. Master Grene might have the same problem.

Mitch will know.

She walked around the lemon . . . no, the *Citrus* . . . with proprietary interest. It was exactly what she wanted. Master Grene's suggestion of artwork and lettering pleased her. She looked at the contact details he'd handed over.

Might as well.

She called the number, and someone picked up almost immediately.

"Greetings . . . Over Here B and B, or Thymelines Gallery."
The voice was pleasant.

"May I speak to Master Kris Peckerdale?" she asked.

"You already are. How may I help?"

"My name's Queenie Hart. Someone suggested you might do some artwork and lettering for my van. I trade as Queen of Tarts."

The man said, "Where are you, Ms Hart? Or is it Mistress Hart?"

"Queenie is fine. I'm near Fiddle Bay in New South Wales."

"Okay. Would you like me to come over to discuss the job?"

"Yes . . . you'd come through the cove gate?"

He laughed. "Not on your life. I'll come through the castle bridge gate like a civilised man."

"Okay . . . I'm going down to Sydney on Friday. I could meet you somewhere."

"How about near the fairy gardens at Windhill? Or wait — there's a café called the Dark Room," he suggested. "There's parking behind. Ring ahead and talk to Flick Dark. Tell her you're meeting Kris Peckerdale, and she'll wish your van in for you."

"Yes. About . . ."

"Two-thirty at the Dark Room," he said.

"Okay. I'll be there. My van —"

" — is a light-yellow Citroën, I expect," he said, laughing. "My nephew has mentioned it. He's been looking for *just* the right person to trust it to."

The phone call ended, and Queenie had another siege of the *what just happened* feeling.

She was still wondering what on earth she'd agreed to — and why — when Mitch came home.

He parked Ethel next to the Citrus and came to hug Queenie. She relaxed into his arms. The odd Master Grene was right. It was nice to feel explody with love, and safe at the same time. "Fixer . . . I'm in a fix."

"Again? Do you need a naked pixie man in a high state of readiness for your pleasures?"

"Oh, *you*. Yes! That's exactly what I need."

"Just as well there's one available, then." He scooped her off her feet, carried her into The Belfry and up the steps without breaking stride.

"Clothes off?"

She nodded, bemused. The last man who had carried her with such effortless grace was James . . . but then her ankles had been howling with pain, so she hadn't been quite able to appreciate it.

Her clothes vanished. So did Mitch's.

"Nice trick," she said.

"I think so."

He sat on the bed. "If you want to face me . . ."

Queenie took the hint, scrambling down and then sitting in his lap with her legs around his hips.

"One naked pixie man . . ."

"Oooooh!" she said.

"Now for the recovery," Mitch said cheerfully after a short and active interval. They lay together with her head on his shoulder. "Let's talk about your fix," he said.

"You just fixed that in spectacular fashion," she said, laughing.

"There's something else, though."

"Hmm. Your cousin came."

"I thought he must have. You had that stunned look. I don't know him all that well, but he certainly has an effect."

"I liked him," she said, having decided she really did. "He's verra attractive."

"Oh?"

"Hackles down, pixie man."

He relaxed. "You're taking that van?"

"Yes." She told him her doubts about the price.

"I expect he wanted you to have it. Odd lad, isn't he?"

"Lad! He's quite a lot older than you . . . or so he said."

"Yes. Not sure what's going on with him. It's the bane of his life, apparently. He still gets carded regularly."

"Did you know he's married?"

Mitch chuckled. "I should say so. He told me when I called him."

"He didn't give me any paperwork, but he did recommend someone to paint the van . . . and I'm meeting *him* on Friday, in Sydney, at two-thirty. My parents are calling in here on Thursday afternoon, and Mum's going to be at a conference all day Friday, so I thought I might meet Dad in Sydney . . . but I also have to get to Branok and Gillan St Ives to get my nest egg back in my normal account. And then I have to pay Master Grene and maybe Master Peckerdale if I decide to go ahead with the painting."

"I see." Mitch tickled the underside of her breast.

Queenie said, despairingly, "I have no idea how I'm going to handle all that."

"I can fix that for you. Look." He conjured a notepad and his wooden pen.

"As soon as I've had you again . . . which will be very soon, because I want you focused on me rather than my *verra attractive* and somewhat crazy cousin . . . call Master St Ives and see what time he and his minx can meet you—and where. Keep the time away from your two-thirty meeting with Master Peckerdale—is that Kris Peckerdale, by the way?"

"Yes."

"Okay. He'll be on time. Call the bank and make an appointment to fit in with the other appointments—you might meet your cousins there.

"Got that?"

"Ye-es."

"With those times in play, you can arrange things with your dad on Thursday and set a time and place to meet on Friday. Give yourself a bit of wiggle room. Then, depending on the outcome of those appointments, you might stay the night in Sydney or come home. If you need to stay the night, I'll drive down — and we can go through the gate and stay with Mum and Dad."

Queenie sat up and eyed him with wonder. "Can you run that by me again?"

Mitch ran through it again.

"Alternatively, you might organise to meet them all — bank manager included — at the same venue at the same time. Sort your business and then go off somewhere with your dad. Then, restore him to your mum when she finishes at her conference. Depending on how you feel, call me a couple of hours beforehand and let me know if you're coming home. If not, I can come to you, and we'll take your parents to dinner where I shall formally ask for your hand."

"You'll do *what*?"

"No?"

"I'm emancipated."

"I know that, darling heart. I should have said, where I'll happen to mention I would quite like to marry you."

"What about James?"

"Obviously, you'll have to marry him too. I can't offer to be best man at your wedding . . . unless we can somehow manage to be Pronounced at midnight on the last day of September, but then — drat it! He'll get to enjoy *my* honeymoon."

"Stop! Stop! You're doing my head in!"

Mitch went silent for a few seconds, and Queenie wondered if she'd offended him.

Then he said, "How about this, then. You marry *him* on the

first of October. That way, you get a clear month together. You can marry *me* on the first of September. We also get a month together before the changeover. Does that suit your sense of equity?"

"Bigamy's illegal."

"Technically, it's not bigamy. Even if it was . . . fay priests take the *many rooms* clause very seriously. They'd much rather countenance bigamy than adultery, so they call it *special circumstances* and toss us into matrimony with alacrity. There's one teg man who is especially good at it."

"What's a teg?"

Mitch said, "Haven't you finished reading that *Orders of the Fay* series yet?"

"I haven't got the last two volumes. Jonquil Lemon Orange said she'd send them when they were available."

"Jonquil Lemon Orange."

"It really *is* her name. Glory . . . what is my name going to be? Queenie Hart-Kingsolver-Stuart? Queenie Hakist? Queenie Ha-Stu-King?"

Mitch laughed. "It's up to you. Maybe we can consult Father Dai."

"Is he the teg?"

"Yes. Tegs are mostly dark haired and slim. They like music and daffodils and they grow leeks . . . serious folk, and as honest as elves. Not a great many this side of the gates."

"I see."

"Phew!" Mitch sighed. "After all that Fixing, I need something to calm me down. Will you do the honours?"

He took Queenie's hand and guided it south.

"You do indeed need calming," she said, and she proceeded to attend to it.

At the back of her mind she noted that she'd just received a kind of proposal of marriage.

Their session was going beautifully when it was

interrupted by Ayesha jumping up on the bed and patting Mitch's face.

Queenie was so shocked that she rolled off the bed.

Ayesha jumped down, but instead of spitting her triumph, she purred warmly, and rubbed her cheek against Queenie's.

Mitch peered down at them, smiling. "Two queens," he said.

Queenie said, "There's room for just *one* queen in this bedroom, moggy," but before she could take steps to eject the ice queen, an idea presented itself. She already had a Queen of Hearts tart, made with a glowing red heart in the centre. Why not complete the set?

"I've thought of three more tarts," she said to Mitch.

"Tell me." He patted the bed, and Queenie got back in. Ayesha chased the stained-glass reflections on the floor.

"I can do the Queen of Spades, with a black spade shape made of liquorice or black currant jelly."

"Black currant," Mitch said. "It'll go with your red Queen of Hearts."

"That's the idea. It can have the same cream custard base. The next one—"

"King of Clubs?" Mitch asked.

"Yes! Blackberry jelly or black cherry on the custard base."

"Black cherry. Blackberry might be a bit bland. Crimped pastry?"

"Yes, following the same recipe as Queen of Hearts except for the centre."

"You could add chocolate or coffee."

"Coffee."

"Add chocolate to the black currant one then."

Queenie propped herself up on pillows. "Just who is inventing these tarts?"

"You are my love. I'm just making suggestions."

"If I'm blending two flavours for Spades and Clubs, I might

modify Hearts to include another flavour. What goes with strawberry?"

"Red currant? Raspberry?"

"I'll test both. That leaves the King of Diamonds. Red currant and . . ."

"Cherry brandy?"

"Perfect, if I can get it to set . . . and I can add a good port to the Queen of Hearts instead of the raspberry."

Mitch said, "These are going to be somewhat *expensive* tarts."

"Verra, but the wicked auld mannie will expect the verra best."

Queenie blinked. Someone . . . Andy or Dellion . . . had said the sight of her brought out Oliver's outrageous side. It seemed to her that Oliver possibly had the same effect on her.

She laughed, excited and delighted in equal measure. "The auld diel will verra likely say the Queen is no' a new tart . . . Och, never mind. I'll hae to come up wi' a bonus."

She stroked his chest. "I'm planning a honey tart called The Beeman, and I wondered if your dad would let me have some of his honey."

"We can see about that on Friday," Mitch said.
Friday was clearly going to be a busy day.

CHAPTER FOURTEEN: WEE JANET

Queenie Hart, November 17th, 2021

Liberty and Shane arrived on Thursday, an hour and a half before Queenie expected them.

"We made good time," Shane said as he hugged her hello. He stood back and looked her over. "You look well, love."

"I *am* well."

The flush in her cheeks had as much to do with her very recent activity in the bedroom as it did with her health.

Thank goodness for a man who can dress me in a second.

"Come on in and meet Mitch. He's got a job on shortly, but he'll be back in an hour or so."

She had told herself she didn't need her parents' approval of her living arrangements, but that didn't keep her from holding her breath as she led the way into the narthex. She so hoped Liberty wouldn't say something cutting about people living in converted churches.

Liberty, though, seemed to be in a conciliatory mood. She admired the economical use of space inside The Belfry, and she asked Queenie about the history of the place. Fortunately, Queenie had read an article in a vintage copy of the *Stradevarious* detailing the early days of the old church, so she could answer her mother's questions with a degree of certainty.

"We had a look at your website. You *have* been busy," Liberty said.

Queenie looked back over the three months since she'd made her move to Kirk Circle. "I have . . . and now I have The

Belfry for as long as I want, as long as I pay the rent."

"I trust your landlord is more civil than the last one," Liberty said. "*Not known at this address* indeed."

Queenie considered Oliver. "He has his moments, but he *wants* me to have what I want. That's the difference."

Shane had wandered over to examine the table in the main room. He was down on his knees, peering at it. Queenie heard him give a long, low whistle.

"What's up, Dad? *Please* don't say you've found wood-worm or — or dry rot."

I'm sure The Belfry wouldnae allow that.

"Not termites?" Liberty said. "Queenie, didn't you have this place inspected?"

"Of course I did." Queenie crossed her fingers. After all, Oliver *had* done an inspection when he came to unward the door.

"I was just looking at this table," Shane said. "It looks as if it was made from a single piece of timber . . . but that's not . . ." He went on muttering to himself, crawling about and running his fingers over the legs. "It's an amazing piece of work."

Before Queenie could say she had never noticed anything unusual about the table, Mitch came down from the mezzanine level, fresh and cheerful, with Ayesha riding on his shoulder.

"Hello, Ms Hart. Lovely to meet you. Is it in order to give you a hug?"

"It is since you had the courtesy to ask first," Liberty said.

Queenie removed Ayesha and put her on a chair. She watched her lover hug her mother.

Let's hope she thinks his bouquet-des-fees *is just washing powder.*

Liberty stepped back, eyeing Mitch uncertainly.

Oh-oh. She knows.

Liberty cleared her throat. "Shane, come out from that

table. Mitchell is here."

Shane crawled out, got up and brushed himself down. He held out his hand to Mitch. "Nice to meet you properly, son," he said. "Mitchell Kingsolver, right?"

Mitch agreed that he was. "I have to get to work, but I'll be back soon. I'd love to take you out for a beer."

Shane said, "Sounds like a plan. Lib?"

"I might stay back and have a chat with Queenie. By the way, can you get her present? I think I left it on our bed."

Shane went out with Mitch to the motorhome, then returned with a package which he put down on the table. "I'm going to work with Mitch. He reckons he just has to shuttle a couple of passengers, so there's plenty of room for me."

He ducked out again.

Liberty said, "And he's gone." She flicked her fingers like a magician.

Queenie braced herself. "Good to see you, Mum."

"You, too." Her eyes sharpened and focused on Queenie's neck. "Striking necklace."

"I think so." Cursing herself for not making sure the thistle gaud was hidden under her shirt, Queenie came to show her mother.

Liberty picked it up and turned it to examine the back of the thistle. Since the back was as fully carved as the front, she presumably didn't learn much. Her eyebrows rose.

"This is unusual. Whatever is it made of?"

"The stone is something called heather gem."

"Lab created?"

"Natural."

"I've not heard of that."

"It comes from a place called Heather Island. It's quite old — it belonged to Mitch's great-grandmother."

Liberty let go of the gaud and Queenie tucked it away. "That's quite a gift."

"That's what I thought. Mitch's mum said she hadn't worn it in decades, so she wanted me to have it."

Liberty said, thoughtfully, "You did say it was serious between you and Mitchell."

"Yes." She didn't mention Mitch's proposal. She thought he wanted to bring that up himself.

Liberty picked up the package and handed it to Queenie. "Only a couple of weeks late."

Queenie opened it slowly.

Not a book . . . surely not an electrical appliance.

The thing was wrapped in tissue paper which fell clear as she took it out of the box.

"Mum, it's beautiful!"

Her mother looked relieved. "We hoped you'd like it. It's antique . . . eighteenth century."

Queenie ran her fingers over the curves of the pink marble pestle and mortar. The date — 1797 — was incised in the marble.

"Two hundred years older than I am," Queenie observed.

"That's why it seemed appropriate," her mother said.

The mortar was impressive in size — far bigger than the small one she used to grind spices.

"This is grand! I can grind up so much more! I'll put it in the kitchen."

Liberty followed Queenie through the divider into the kitchen where she looked about with interest. "This is industrial sized. Did you remodel?"

"No, Oliver — my landlord — did the conversion himself. His wife liked baking and Oliver likes eating, so it worked for them both. They lived here for a while."

"Lucky for you, considering your business," Liberty said.

"Verra."

Liberty winced.

Queenie sighed. "Oops."

"You said Mitchell's mother gave you that necklace?"

"Yes. That is, she gave it to her son to give to me."

Nice save . . .

It was James who had presented the necklace.

Ayesha swanned into the kitchen and chirruped at Queenie.

"Aye, moggy, he'll be back in a wee while." She bent and picked up the cat.

Liberty pretended not to notice the slip.

How odd . . . Since when does she pretend?

"Queenie—what you were asking the other day. I don't think there's any way of finding out much more. I did look out the photo of Uncle Don, but it's hard to say exactly what the odd eye effect is. He *might* just have been looking into the sun, or maybe light reflected from the bowl in front of him." She rummaged in her bag and brought out an old black and white print, faded and soft around the edges. "This is the original. I have a digitised copy, if you prefer."

"I'd like to have this, if you can spare it."

"Not much good to me," Liberty said.

Queenie put Ayesha down and gazed at the picture. The man was wearing a kilt, although she couldn't tell the colour. His eyes did look odd—a silvery shade, but his hair seemed to be dark. He stood beside a chair, leaning one arm on a pillar containing some liquid in a bowl. Two women sat side by side to his left, wearing skirts and blouses with jackets. Their hair was dressed back and confined in what Queenie thought was called a snood, and they wore tiny hats . . . little more than a shaped strip of stiffened cloth with a bunch of beaded flowers and a short veil. Another man stood on the other side of the women. He was short and round-faced and was looking down at the woman next to him. She had something in her lap . . . maybe a posy.

"This is Mum's Uncle Don," Liberty said, indicating the kilted man. "I believe the woman next to him is his wife— May. They had a son, but he never married. He did have children, I think, but that's a . . . one of those family tales.

"The other man is Jos Southey, my grandmother's husband. Josiah or Jonas . . . not sure. That's Adelaide sitting next to him. You can see she looks a bit like her brother, but her eyes aren't light like his."

"This Jonas is not your grandfather?" Queenie asked.

"Probably not. I did look up a few dates in that digitised newspaper site. Adelaide seems to have met him just before the Second World War . . . that is, they are reported as attending some functions together . . . and they married soon after. That was quite common in those days. I remember him, although I never knew him well. I called him Joshie."

"When was Granny born?"

"I'm not sure — don't look like that. Who goes about asking their mother if she celebrates her birthday on the correct date?"

"Verra true," Queenie said dryly. "You and Dad always call me the day after mine."

Liberty frowned, but not, apparently, in anger.

"I can understand why," Queenie said.

"Mum always claims to be a war baby, but Joshie was away for years . . . actually in the trenches. And there's a baby photo of Mum — a studio shot she gave me years ago when she was in one of her minimalist phases. I don't know if she even knew she gave it to me — it was in a box of old photos and books. Come to think of it, I ought to hand it over to you, since you're the only one of the family with room for storage. Remind me to get it out before we leave."

"I promise I'll look after it."

"No need for promises. If I give it to you, it's yours to do with as you like."

"The photo?" Queenie said.

"Ah, yes. She looks about two or three, standing up in a short frock — tartan with white smocking by the looks of it —

with those hen's bum knickers and little black shoes with a strap. Patent leather, possibly. It's hand coloured, which is what they often did with studio portraits back then. The date on the back is smudged by what looks to me like a thumb-print."

"That's bad luck."

"I'd say luck had nothing to do with it. It was in pencil, and the thumbprint has scuffed up the cardboard as if someone licked her thump or dipped it in water and then *scrubbed*."

"Oh."

Liberty went on, "The studio logo FS and the name Folly Studio is printed — embossed really — on the back of the photo. It's survived well, probably because it's been in a frame. I looked it up and that studio closed in nineteen-forty. There was an article about it. The owner may have enlisted in the army. It doesn't seem to have reopened." She glanced at Queenie. "It's precious little to go on, but you see Adelaide is holding flowers in this photo and Joshie has a white button-hole. I'm pretty sure this one is a wedding picture, and the picture of Mum would predate this by as much as four years."

"You've gone into it . . . thought you weren't interested."

"You are, though, so I found what I could."

"Are you sure the photo is of Granny?"

Liberty laughed. "You wouldn't ask if you saw it. She's standing with one foot turned out and her head on an angle and one arm curved so her hand's on her hip. Very *look at me!* Mum stands that way for photos to this day. Besides, it's got *Wee Janet* written across it."

"*Wee* Janet."

"Yes. As I said, there's very little to go on, especially with Mum conveniently forgetting or refusing to corroborate things she told me years ago. If she *does* predate her mother's wedding to Joshie, then God knows who — or what — her fa-ther was. I'm pretty sure she doesn't know. If Adelaide knew, she wasn't saying. In those days there were plenty of things that were common knowledge, or at least commonly suspected and gossiped about, but never actively confirmed. Families liked to keep their privacy." She sniffed. "If you ask me, we could take a leaf out of their book. All this public geyser-gushing is self-indulgent at best and attention-seeking at worst."

Queenie laughed. "Weren't you just saying Granny should admit to what she told you?"

"That's different. I'm her nearest relative. I'm hardly *public*."

"Verra true."

"So now you know everything I knew and what I could find out. If I were you, I wouldn't spend any more time on this. The trails are just too muddied. You could always ask Mum, if you can get yourself into the retreat, but she's just as likely to look at you sweetly and then try to read your aura."

"I won't, then," Queenie said. "It doesnae matter. Knowing whose blood we carry isnae too important. It's gey obvious *what* blood it is . . ." She dragged her diction back into line. "It looks like two lots of tartan blood have crept into you and me, anyway. If Uncle Don here was brae, then Adelaide was too . . . unless she was a half-sister?"

Liberty shrugged. "She did have big hips."

"You don't," Queenie observed.

"No . . . I look like my dad's family, the Bells. There's a picture of Granny and Granddad Bell in that box somewhere with some of their children. Two of Dad's sisters are dead-ringers for me."

Queenie by now was looking forward to delving into that box, but she stuck to the point. "If Adelaide got Granny from a roll in the heather with a braeman . . . or halfling or some such, the blood would reinforce . . . I think."

Liberty turned out her hands. "Maybe—but there's no

getting around the fact that I'm as human as they come, and Mum—"

Queenie stared at her.

Liberty had the grace to look sheepish. "Mum is as mad as a wet sheep, nine points north of normal, and always was. Not to worry, she and Dad did their best by me. She kept her odd ways under control until I left home. Sheer willpower, I think."

"Does Grandad know anything about this?" Queenie asked.

"If he does, he's not saying. Your Grandad Bell is a quiet pool, a dear man who makes an oyster look gabblesome."

"Nice word, Mum."

"Thank you. I just coined it."

"I know you did *your* best by me, and it was a verra good best," Queenie said. She remembered Branok St Ives giving that same opinion and insulting her into the bargain.

She added, "Thanks, Mum—truly. Now—just one more concession from you, and you might manage to believe in Lassie Haggis."

"In what?"

Queenie explained.

Liberty said, awkwardly, "I never disbelieved in it. I just thought you should be able to control it."

"Funny you should say that. My landlord thinks I should, too. I spent years trying, but this year I've decided not to look on it as a curse . . . as I said. It's a manifestation and supressing it might not be such a good idea."

"What does Mitchell think of it?"

"He accepts it. Anyway, we didn't spend October together, so he didn't get the full effect."

"Oh?"

"Yes. We met in August, and then at the end of September he had to go away for a month. He came back on the first—

seventeen days ago."

"You must have got very close very quickly."

"We did." She considered leaving it at that, but Liberty did appear to be holding an olive branch, so she said, "Mum, if I tell you a bit more about that, can you just accept it? I mean, don't advise me or object, or sigh, or try to analyse it."

"That sounds ominous."

"It's not. Really not."

"I'll do my best."

"Perfect! So—you accept that Lassie Haggis is real. She's not another person . . . she's me . . . but an altered me who shares the same memories but who has different tastes, and a much worse temper. She's impulsive, which I'm not."

Liberty said, "I do accept that. I don't want to, but I do."

"Then please accept that Mitch has something similar also related to October."

"Oh—" Liberty looked alarmed.

"He also has an altered self, but his is far more autonomous. He doesn't look or sound the same."

Liberty screwed up her face.

"Yes?"

"I don't want to admit this. I never mentioned it to *anyone* . . . definitely not your dad, but you look a *tiny* bit different in October. Your eyes. And . . . and your bearing changes. Like a dog . . . I don't mean you look like one, but you react to things no one else hears."

"I never knew that until very recently, but I have a photo taken at Halloween and I saw it . . . I'll show you."

Queenie ran upstairs and grabbed her double frame from the nightstand.

She returned to the kitchen and showed the twin photos to her mother.

Liberty stared unblinkingly at the evidence of what she'd tried for years not to admit. "Yes. That's the look. I used to try not to see it, because it reminded me of Mum at her—forget that."

"That's okay. Anyway, that's Lassie Haggis—in my Queen of Tarts costume at the ball."

"You look—fantastic."

"I do." Queenie grinned, knowing Liberty was using the term advisedly. "Fantastic is how I look in that costume."

She waited for the inevitable question.

Liberty obliged. "Who is this?" She indicated the kilted figure beside the Queen of Tarts.

"That's my Jamie. James Stuart. He's the October laddie, the person who takes over from Mitch." She gazed at him affectionately.

My darling laddie.

She indicated the other picture. "This one is of Mitch and me, taken about fourteen hours after the one of Jamie and me. Same setting, same photographer."

Liberty seemed transfixed.

"Mum?"

"I don't want to say this, but I owe it to you. I can *see*—her—and I can see these two . . ."

"Are different."

"But they're not! They're *the same.* At least, in some degree. Just look at their faces. They're both looking at you in *exactly* the same way—except the one in the kilt has a bit more yearning."

"Aye, they love me. Jamie knew he'd have to leave and he didnae want to go. They—"

Liberty swallowed audibly. "Enough. Queenie, I love you dearly and I accept you as an autonomous person who happens to bear my blood and your dad's. Mitchell seems open and friendly, and I can see he's fond of you. I can also see he's—a fairy. However, I think I've gained as much insight into your situation as I can handle just now. I need time to absorb it. I promise I'll try."

"Thanks, Mum." Queenie gave her a hug.

"Oh, lord," Liberty said into her shoulder. "Your dad's gone off in a bus with a fairy . . . and you *know* how he feels about fairies."

Chapter Fifteen: The Ninth Tart

Queenie Hart, November 17th, 2021

Shane and Mitch returned in time for lunch, after which they went to the pub for the promised drink.

Once they returned, Queenie's parents took their leave.

"Got to book in and sort things for tomorrow," Liberty said.

Shane tore himself away from Queenie's furnishings.

"By the way, Dad," Queenie said.

"What's up, love?"

"I'm going into the city tomorrow . . . giving my new van a spin and meeting someone who might do some paintwork for me. If you're free, we can meet up for a coffee."

"Sounds good to me. Where are you meeting this bloke? Or sheila, as the case might be?"

"Bloke. His name's Kris Peckerdale. We arranged to meet at a café called the Dark Room in the mall at two-thirty. Know it?"

"Can't say I do. Bound to be a lot of new places since we left on our travels."

"I need to phone the proprietor about parking, so I'll get the exact address and text you."

"Righto. You'll have to do any negotiating yourself, mind."

"Well, obviously. I don't expect we'll be long, so I thought you and I could stay on after the meeting and have a catch-up."

"You coming too, Mitch?" Shane asked.

"I have to work, but I could come and meet you all for dinner."

"Grand!" Shane looked genuinely pleased.

Just as the elder pair were about to leave, Queenie called, "I have to meet someone else too to sign some paperwork. I might get them to come to the café too — have the whole thing over in one sitting."

"Sounds like a regular bunfight," Shane said agreeably. He waved out the window and drove off.

"You don't know the half of it, Dad," Queenie said under her breath.

Mitch put his arms around her. "Just what are you cooking up, my own love?"

"I *hope* I'm arranging a loveday. On the other hand, it might be more like the Battle of Agincourt."

"Do you need the Fixer? I could always get Olivier Campania to sub for me here."

"Thanks for the offer. I *am* using one of the models you suggested, but I have to do this myself. It's my responsibility, since I'm arranging it. If it all goes south then that will be bad, but let's look on the bright side. If my ducks won't line up, it might not happen at all."

The Fixer phone rang at that point, and Mitch rolled expressive eyes at Queenie. "Fixer."

Queenie heard an anxious voice quavering on the other end.

Mitch listened, then he said. "Where are you?"

More quavering.

"Okay, I know the place. Go back into the café. Order a pot of tea. Take your time over it. I'll be there in around eighty minutes. Don't worry a bit. It will be okay."

He conjured his Fixer cap and put it on his head. "Bye, my darling love," he said, and seconds later he was in Ethel and driving away.

Queenie went back into The Belfry, where she made some prototype Chloe tarts with fresh ginger and fed Ayesha. In between, she made telephone calls to Flick Dark of the Dark Room, who agreed readily to *wish your van in, lovie,* then to Branok St Ives.

"You're not coming to the office?" he asked.

"I'm not coming by train—I've bought a van. Hence I need to sign out that nest egg. Do you know a café called the Dark Room?"

"Certainly. Gillan and I meet friends there quite often. In fact, we've meeting one of our daughters-by-love there to-morrow . . ."

"What time?"

"After she's finished whatever she's doing . . . we'll wait for her to call."

"I'll be there at two-thirty."

"That will work. Then we go to the bank?"

"I was hoping the manager might come to the café. I was also hoping *you* might ask him. And possibly use just a tiny bit of charm on him."

"You don't ask much, Cousin Queenie Hart."

"Och, I'm verra audacious."

"My word, you are. I don't use charms that way. The term you want is influence, and I will *not* use influence on your bank manager. That's a disgraceful suggestion. My younger son does it occasionally but *only,* so he assures me, if the recipient agrees. He used to be less scrupulous, but now he's a husband and father he has become a model citizen." He paused for a beat and then answered, "And if I believed that, I'd believe in fairies. Oh . . . wait . . ."

"You won't help me, then."

"I didn't say that. I'll call the bank and suggest the manager might take his tea break in a very fine café between two and three and bring the relevant paperwork as a favour to a fellow professional. That's all I'll do. If he won't agree, then we'll go to the bank like anyone else."

"Thanks. I owe you."

"You do. A dozen assorted tarts will suffice. Please also bring an order form. We're having the family at home for Christmas, and a friend might drop in with her man, their daughter, two dogs and a miniature pony and possibly another couple and *their* child plus two more dogs, one of which is civilised and the other of which is certifiable. I shall need fortifying with jam to face that lot."

"How does a family tart sound to you?"

"It sounds delicious. But Queenie, just a hint . . . please don't add any dogfood tarts to your selection. Lady Velvet would be pleased, but Gillan might —"

A yell of outrage suggested Gillan was indeed offended.

Queenie hung up on the cacophony that followed.

She telephoned Flick Dark again and asked to reserve a large table for a possible seven people — only two of whom were entirely human and two of whom didn't get along.

"I'll put you in the private room and ward it for sound," Flick said obligingly.

Queenie thanked her and hung up.

Her plans were as complete as she could make them.

"The Family Tart," she said aloud, distracting herself. "A *big* tart — the size of a family pizza, with twelve different flavours. The tart for sharing."

She beamed, picturing herself serving the prototype to Mitch. She'd bring it to him in bed. She wouldn't tell him about it beforehand. It would be a surprise.

Mitch was home late that day.

It was dark, and Queenie had gone to bed early in preparation for a long and possibly confronting day tomorrow.

She heard Ethel pull in alongside the Citrus. Ayesha had prowled in to join her, curling in a companionable hummock behind Queenie's knees.

The ice queen appeared to have capitulated completely, although Queenie didn't know exactly why.

"Aye, moggy, wish ye could tell me, in case I need to use the alchemy again tomorrow."

Alchemy. Mitch had used that word to describe the ceasefire between himself and his brother.

She was still awake when Mitch came in. He leaned down and kissed her. "Queenie, love?"

"Greet you," she said into the dark.

Mitch moved his hand . . . she felt the breeze of it over her cheek, and the lights came on.

She blinked. "What's that smell . . . oh!" She sat up. Her grandmother's Cloisonne vase rested on the nightstand, overflowing with pale yellow floribunda roses.

"Oh — *Mitch*!" She leaned over to inhale. The roses, of a variety she didn't know, had the true tea rose perfume with an undertone of lemon. "These are so beautiful. What are they called?"

"Can't you guess?"

"Lemon?"

"Close . . . *Ami de Citron* . . . Lemon Friend, in other words. The parents are Reine de l'amour and Lemon Zest. The first one is pink and the second one is bright yellow. Don't ask me why their offspring is lemon cream."

Queenie said, "Is this to celebrate my new van?"

"Yes . . . in a way. The client who needed help today is associated with a company called V-S Roses. After I got her out of her fix, I asked her if they had anything fragrant and pale yellow with culinary uses, and she came up with this one. She says she likes it for making candied rose petals, rosewater and rose sugar." He paused, and then added, "It's the wrong time of the year to plant out rose bushes, but I bought one of these in a pot which you can keep as a pot plant until winter if you like. I thought you might want a tart-creation garden."

Queenie went on drawing in the delicious scent and visualising the tart she could make with rosewater and candied roses.

"It will be called the Lemon Sunshine—one of my new Rose series," she said.

Mitch didn't ask what she meant. He knew.

He moved away from the bed and pulled out his phone.

"Queenie."

"Mm?" She looked up.

Snap.

"Mitch . . . I'm not dressed!"

He poked about and finally located his gallery. Then, he wordlessly held out the phone.

Somehow, by fluke or design, he'd caught her bare shoulders rising over the roses, with the thistle gaud catching the light.

He turned it back to peer at the screen. "I'm going to have this one framed on my side of the bed."

He laid the phone on the chair he had been using as a nightstand, got naked, and climbed into bed.

The light went out, and Queenie lay down. The scent of roses bathed the room and Ayesha sneezed.

Queenie said, into the dark, "Mitch, only two men have ever given me flowers."

"James gave you some. I remember. I'm not competing."

"I know. He gave me freesias and violets and now I have roses. You both chose perfumed flowers in some of my favourite colours."

He put his arms around her. "Busy day tomorrow, my love."

"Tell me about it. I wonder if I have time to make some candied roses before I drive down to the city."

"Plenty of time. Have you thought what you want on your van?"

"I have a few ideas, but I thought I'd see what Master Peckerdale recommends. I looked him up and found quite a lot of information—he's indie-famous as a fantasy artist, so I hope he can come up with something magical."

Mitch said, "Why not take your Queen of Tarts photo—maybe photograph it on your phone—to show him? And some tarts if you have some to spare. He might be able to do a sort of cornucopia effect."

In the back of Queenie's mind, the huge Family Tart was joined by its companion—the Cornucopia, spilling over with fruit and marzipan and candied flowers.

She said, "I'm taking some for Branok . . . he says I owe him."

"Why?"

"I asked him to use influence on my bank manager—just to get him to agree to meet us away from the bank."

"I doubt if that went down well," Mitch said.

"It didn't, but he said he'd *ask*. Hence the tarts. Mind you, he also said one of his sons uses influence sometimes, but only on people who want it. Whyever would anyone want to be influenced?"

Mitch said, "I believe it can be useful for some people—a bit like hypnosis. Maybe that's what he meant."

"Maybe. Anyway, he wants tarts, and he's going to get them. I'll certainly pack another dozen or so to bribe the bank manager and Master Peckerdale. Good idea."

"I don't think bribing them is a good idea."

She laughed. "Bad choice of words. Am I allowed to *sweeten the deal*?"

"Yes. Don't forget the shortbread option."

"I hadn't thought of that. I need to update my courtesy cards."

"Are you too sleepy for—"

"Never," she said, laughing and rolling on top of him.

"Oops," she added as Ayesha hissed and leaped off the bed. "Sorry, moggy."

Mitch kissed her.

Making love in the rose-scented dark was a sensory delight. It was only when she was almost asleep that she remembered Mitch hadn't referred to his proposal.

Chapter Sixteen: The Dark Room

Queenie Hart, November 18th, 2021

Queenie made candied rose petals and gloated over the potted rose Mitch had left on the big table. He had added a catalogue, and he suggested she might order more roses when it was time to plant them.

In her mind's eye, she saw a glorious garden around The Belfry, encompassing not only roses, but violets, marigolds, borage and other eatable flowers. She'd grow soft fruit and berries, and make a herb garden.

She acquired Peck Grene's number from Mitch and telephoned him to arrange for delivery of the Chloe tarts.

"Where shall I put them so you can get a fix?" she asked.

There was no use using Oliver's table, because Peck had never been inside The Belfry.

"That place you call Vicar-ville."

"Yes?"

"There's a wooden crate there."

"Yes. I sit on it when I go to visit them."

"Use a tart box like the one I got from you and put it on the crate."

"Okay. Fifteen minutes."

"The ones you gave me before were good."

"Which did you like best?"

"The green ones."

He meant the Irish Shamrocks.

"Thanks," she said. She packed his tarts, adding a couple

of extra Shamrocks, and waited at Vicar-ville for him to con-jure them away.

Ayesha wandered up and wrapped her tail around Queenie's ankles.

"Hello, moggy."

The ice queen gave a companionable mew.

The tart box blinked out of existence.

Queenie wondered how much elapsed time was involved when the fay conjured. Was it truly instantaneous? Was Peck Grene unpacking his box of tarts already?

The hours stretched.

Queenie wished she'd arranged her meeting for the morn-ing. She didn't want to be waiting about in the city, so she tried out her new pestle and mortar.

Ayesha came in, then headed off for the belltower.

I ought to see to those bells.

She went to the bedroom and inhaled the rich rose scent. The Cloisonne vase had a muted pattern that didn't detract from the roses.

She remembered James had taken odds and ends out of the vase and put them in a drawer and went to check.

Yes, there they were. Great-Grandmother Victoria Grant's bracelet was too small for Queenie's wrist. Granny Vic must have been tiny.

That reminded her of the other two gifts she'd inherited from her great-grandmothers ... Great-Granny Elizabeth Mack's clock and Great-Granny Adelaide Southey's painting.

It occurred to Queenie that although she'd seen that paint-ing just about every day since childhood, she had no idea of its provenance. She returned to the bedroom, where it hung on the wall above her wooden chest.

James' basket of memories rested beside the chest, and Queenie opened the loosely-fitting cover and tucked in a cor-ner of the soft blanket. The little carved box was tipped over, and she straightened it. It had a lid, but it wouldn't open.

She looked up at the painting. It was a landscape, and she examined it. It had rolling hills painted with soft purple, and a few brighter splashes. A low stone house cuddled into the fold of a hill, and grey smudges suggested a stone wall surrounding its garden. There was something else that might have been a streak of paint above the wall, and a sort of puddle . . .

Weird.

Queenie fetched her magnifying glass from the drawer. She moved it over the house and wall and stopped at the streak and the puddle.

She laughed. The smudge was a grey dog leaping over the wall. The puddle resolved into a litter of puppies, playing in the grass.

She unhooked the picture and looked at the back of the frame. It was discoloured with age. Carefully, she swivelled the clips and gently pried out the cardboard backing.

Oops.

The cardboard wasn't a backing. It was the card on which the picture was painted. A paper frame had been laid over the card between the painting and the glass to give the effect of matting. It fell away, clung by one corner, and then dropped onto the bed.

Queenie picked it up to replace it, but she stopped when she saw the paper frame had masked the edges of the painting.

Underneath, the paint was brighter, but along the bottom edge the purple foreground faded to cream to allow for a signature written in purple ink.

Adelaide Breck Mulholland 1938.

So, Great-Granny Adelaide was the painting's creator, unless this was another person with the same first name.

I wonder if Mum knows . . . Have I time to give her a call, or will she be on a panel or something?

She glanced at Great-Granny Elizabeth Mack's clock.

"Crikey!" It was — she was going to be late.

She'd been going to dress to impress, but she fled down the steps to the kitchen.

She crammed tarts into boxes, grabbed her keys and her besom, and tore out to the Citrus.

A note on the windscreen surprised her, and she snatched it off.

Remember to call me in plenty of time if we're having dinner with Shane and Liberty. I'll feed Ayesha. Love you. Mitch.

Immediately, she felt steadier.

She remembered she hadn't texted Shane the Dark Room address, so she did that.

He responded with a *See you soon.*

Queenie drove down the coast and into the city. It was a good while since she'd driven so far, but the Citrus was responsive and well-behaved. She followed her GPS into the heart of the city, and thence to the Dark Room. As Flick Dark had directed, she parked in a five-minute spot and sent a text.

Ninety seconds later, a young blonde woman rushed up. "Hitch over, lovie. I'll park for you."

Bemused, Queenie hitched over.

The blonde drove into a car park behind the mall. It appeared to be crammed full, but a parking spot magically opened up for the Citrus.

The blonde turned to smile at her. "See you inside. By the way, I'm Flick Dark."

She smelled of marzipan.

Queenie collected her bag and her besom, then followed Flick into the café.

"Bran St Ives said you're a pastrycook," Flick said.

"Yes. I trade as Queen of Tarts."

"I'm a confectioner, so we might be able to put some business in one another's way. Talk later. Meanwhile . . ." She opened a door and indicated a small room lit by a skylight. It had a low table surrounded by comfortable chairs.

"I'll get Chas—my husband—to bring you some menus later. I'll send the rest of your party when they come in."

Flick smiled and was gone.

Queenie looked at her phone. *Two-thirty on the dot.*

She had barely sat down when the door opened and two men came in. One was in his late twenties or early thirties and the other considerably older.

The younger one had on a Dark Room T-shirt, so Queenie took a punt on the other one being the artist.

He was old enough to be the startling Peck Grene's uncle.

She got to her feet. "Master Peckerdale?"

The man nodded. "Queenie Hart." He took her offered hand. "You might want to put down the besom," he added.

"Oh—" Queenie propped it against the wall. "I don't know why I brought it." She added, "Do you want to look at the van?"

"I'm familiar with it. My nephew has been tinkering with it for months. I'm glad he finally found someone he deemed worthy to own it." He had a pleasant voice, and he smelled of bitter thyme. "It will be okay, you know," he said.

"What will? The van?"

"That will be, yes. Only one vehicle has ever dared to defeat my nephew, and that belongs to my great-nephew's wife. We all love Josefa dearly, but she and vehicles just don't get along."

"What did you mean then?" she asked.

Kris Peckerdale turned his full attention on her. "Peck informed me you're likely to wed with Mitchell Kingsolver."

"Oh, did he!"

"Don't take it amiss, Ms Hart. Since Peck discovered the delights of wedded life with the charming and surprisingly tolerant Chloe, he wants everyone to have the same satisfaction. Fix-it pixie, you see."

"I take it you're not," Queenie said.

"Great bogle no!" He actually made a warding-off gesture. "One of those in the family is *quite* enough. My niece Ryl is a fairy godmother, so we're all well used to being fussed at and — er — fixed whether we want it or not. I'm the quiet one in the family. The dull one. At least, I used to think so. *Are* you going to marry Mitchell?"

"Nothing's arranged yet," Queenie said. "Master Peckerdale, why are we talking about my love life? We're supposed to be talking about designs for my van."

"And you think this is none of my business."

"Frankly —"

"It's not, obviously. Beaman Kingsolver is related somewhere to my grandfather Gard Tillien. I've met him now and then — and his wife. I don't know Mitchell at all well. Oddly enough, I have spent time with James."

"Och, weel ye get on wi' it mun!" Queenie found she was clutching the besom again.

Kris Peckerdale peered at her. "Extraordinary. Might I talk to Queenie, lassie?"

"Ye *are*, ye sleekit —" Queenie choked and almost flung the besom away. "I do beg your pardon."

"No need. I'll stop beating about the bush and say my piece and then we can get back to discussing your van. It's nothing to do with me, but if you were hesitating about wedding Mitchell on account of James, then maybe I can set your mind at rest. I've been married to my colleen, Calypso, for many years, but I've been acquainted with her other self, Mistress Calico, for even longer. She presents as a delightful calico queen. We're very good friends. Clearly, your situation is a bit different, since Mitchell and James are both man-form, rather than colleen and cat, but it *will* be all right." He gave her a sudden grin. "If nothing else, you'll never be bored. Now, let's get to work."

The abrupt change of subject unsettled Queenie, but she

pulled her mind into gear.

What is it wi' folk telling me to wed my fixer and my laddie?

Kris conjured a sketchbook and handed it to her.

"These are some things I sketched in different styles. Let me know if anything takes your eye. Did you bring ideas to show me?"

Queenie woke up her phone and located her gallery. "There are photos of tarts, and of me in my Halloween costume. Mitch suggested a cornucopia effect."

He grinned. "Turn to page nine."

Queenie turned. He'd drawn a giant cornucopia somewhat sideways as if being blown by a gale, with round shapes suggestive of tarts spilling out.

Beneath it was lettering, *Queen of Tarts,* with the *Q* made into a crown and the *T* into a sceptre.

"On the next page there are some scrolls of fruit and flowers—roses, violets, cherries, apples—they'd all be in colour, and now I've seen this costume, I can use those tones for the lettering."

He watched her turn pages, then he conjured a new book and outlined the Citrus. He shaded it in and then conjured a set of ink pens and rapidly drew the lettering, scrollwork and the main cornucopia. "Too fussy?" he asked.

"Maybe a bit—"

"I agree. How about this—" He started again, making bigger lettering and cutting back on the curlicues.

At some point, the younger man brought in menus.

"Thanks Chas—green tea for me and herb bread—Queenie?"

"The same." She watched his flying pencil.

He conjured a paint box and lined up dabs of paint. "These shades. Oh and—" Another sketch book of lettering skipped into view.

The waiter, Chas, caught Queenie's eye. "Never gets old, seeing them throw stuff about, does it?"

"No."

"I assume you're like me and can't do it?"

"I'm mostly human."

"Just don't get in the way of her besom," Kris said, beckoning an ink pot into being.

Chas laughed and withdrew.

Kris went off in another frenzy of sketching. He skidded the page to Queenie, with the graphics cut back again and the lettering larger. "Better?"

"Aye. Ye clever wee mannie, that's right bonnie."

"Let's settle on that then. Ah—do put that besom away."

She pushed it towards the wall.

"What day will suit you for me to work on it?"

Queenie went through her days. "Market, deliveries for the Chess-Nuts . . . Wednesday? But you won't want to stay here that long."

"Best I go home and get Peck to do the honours. Park the van back at your place where he put it originally, and I'll have him get it to me and then back when I'm done. Trust me to work without supervision?"

"Aye. Ye're a pixie man."

He conjured most of the papers away, retaining one book. Chas brought the food and Kris ate with one hand while he made more rapid sketches. He spun these to Queenie. "Calypso," he said, indicating a woman wearing one black and one white stocking and very little else. "She's an exotic dancer. This one is Calico." He tapped a drawing of an exquisite little cat. "Our son Corin and his betrothed."

"She's a pisky," Queenie said.

"Halfling, but she threw hard to her dad's side. This is our daughter, and her—well, not sure what. I suspect she'll turn up one day and say she's married him and they're having triplets." He put his head on one side. "She's a strange one, our Jin, but I reckon he's got her measure."

Queenie said, "Do you do portraits?"

"Not a lot. I specialise in fantasy landscapes with fig-
ures . . . which of course aren't fantasy at all. I do sketches,
obviously, but mainly for my own amusement." He drew a
quick picture of a man apparently fleeing from some geese.
"Like this. You wouldn't believe the things I see sometimes."

Queenie remembered the bats, boiling out of the belltower.
She believed it.

The door opened again, and Branok and Gillan came in.
Branok said, "Hello, Cousin Queenie. The bank manager will
be here in ten. You owe me tarts."

Kris said, "Greet you, Master St Ives. Mistress Gillan.
And — are we going to be graced with Lady Velvet this afternoon?"

"No," Gillan said, "but she sends her greetings to Mistress
Calico." She turned to Branok. "Order for me, will you, Bran?
Queenie . . ." She gave her a hug. "How's the tribe?" she
asked, over her shoulder.

"Noisy, contentious, and implausible," Kris said.

"Normal, then. And Richenda?"

"Betrothed to Corin."

"I see." Gillan glanced at Queenie. "Richenda — ah, I see
Kris has drawn her for you — she's a connection of Bran's."

Queenie began to feel dizzy.

The door opened yet again, and the bank manager with
whom they'd dealt back in September stepped in.

He looked bemused and a bit uneasy. "Ah — Ms Hart? Mister and Missus St Ives I know, but who — " He discreetly indicated Kris.

Kris said, through a mouthful, "Hello. Don't mind me. I'm
about to leave — " He looked at the table as a large platter of
tapas slid discreetly into view. "On second thoughts, I'll stay.
I'm Kristos Peckerdale, by the way."

The bank manager seemed a little pale. "When — how — "

"Splendid service here," Kris said. "You hardly see the waiting staff." He reached for the platter.

"My husband will be back shortly," Gillan said kindly. "Have you brought the paperwork, Mister Farnham?"

The bank manager delved in his briefcase.

Branok came back. "I ordered tea and coffee. Mister Farnham?"

"I have an electronic transfer set up, Ms Hart. Are you still prepared to do as we — agreed?"

He glanced at Kris.

"Yes, we want to take the whole amount less one hundred dollars out of this account . . ." She handed him a slip of paper. "And I want to put it into *this* one." She handed him a card.

"And you are agreeable? Mister St Ives?"

"Certainly."

"Missus St Ives?"

"Yes."

"No duress? You are doing this of your own free will?"

"*Aye*," Queenie blurted.

She had somehow got hold of the besom again, and she pushed it away.

The bank manager looked nervous. "Then, sign here — and here — and here — " He indicated the places. "Mister and Missus St Ives, you agree to return the whole sum, less one hundred dollars, to Ms Hart to be put into an account for her sole use and benefit?"

"We do," Gillan said. "But leave the joint account open — right, Queenie?"

"Yes. We'll use it again next September. Kris, how much will I owe you for the paintwork?" Queenie asked.

The bank manager cleared his throat.

Kris said, "I'll send you an account. My nephew said I was to give you a good deal, and so I will. Otherwise, he'll be starting to *fix* me—"

The bank manager cleared his throat again. "*If* you're all ready . . ."

Chas came in with a tray of tea and coffee.

While he was unloading it, there was a tap on the door.

"Come in, darling," Gillan called.

A slim young woman came in. She was delicately fair, and a short silver earring proclaimed her as a pisky miss. She wore a lot of silver pins and chains, and the baby carrier she had strapped to her chest was decorated with silver badges.

Gillan embraced her and cooed to the baby. "Githa, this is Queenie Hart, a young relative of Bran's, and thus of Zennor's and Cammie's." She beckoned to Queenie. "This is Zennor's wife, Githa and our granddaughter, Camelot," she said. She added, "Sit down darling . . . I'll take Cammie."

"Excuse me," the bank manager said.

Gillan signed the paper, examined the tablet he showed her, and nodded.

Branok raised one brow at Queenie and did the same.

"Now, Ms Hart."

The baby waved a small fist and her mother fished her out of the carrier and put her into Gillan's arms.

Flick came back in. "The other member of your party is here," she said.

The bank manager looked distracted.

Kris poured another cup of tea. "I hope you brought some tarts," he said to Queenie.

"I did, but I'm not sure . . ." Queenie glanced apologetically at Flick.

"That's fine, sweet. I'll get you a serving plate and—oh, sorry. Do come in." She pushed the door wider, and Shane stepped into the room.

Chapter Seventeen: The Tenth Tart

Queenie Hart, November 18th, 2021

Shane froze, his gaze skittering between the people in the room.

Queenie held her breath.

She got to her feet, and she stepped forward to take Shane's arm. "Hi, Dad. Come and sit by me."

She got him into a seat that appeared suddenly between hers and Kris'. She wondered which of the fairies in the room was responsible for that.

The baby's wide eyes never blinked. Presumably little Camelot St Ives was used to people tossing chairs about.

Queenie said, "Dad, this is Kris. He's doing some artwork on my new van. Kris, this is my dad, Shane."

Kris gave his placid smile. "I'll be getting out of your hair as soon as I've sampled your daughter's fabled tarts."

A platter materialised in front of Queenie. She hoisted up her bag and said, "Gillan, will you—"

"I will, lovie," Flick said.

She took charge of the tarts and piled them onto the platter.

Then she left, closing the door behind her.

"This is Mister Farnham, my bank manager . . . I'm not sure if you know him?"

"Don't think so," Shane said.

Mister Farnham was sweeping things into his briefcase. "All done," he muttered.

"Not staying for afternoon tea? Then take a couple of

tarts," Gillan said, proffering the platter.

He chose a couple at random.

"Take an order form as well," Gillan said. "Queenie, may I?"

"Sure. In here." Queenie chucked her thumb at her bag and pushed the besom away.

Gillan handed a form to the bank manager who nodded, took it, and fled.

"What a strange man," Githa St Ives said, gazing after him.

Kris gave a sudden crack of laughter.

Queenie resumed her introductions. "Dad, this is Githa St Ives. Her baby is called Camelot, and she's a connection of ours because her dad's Zennor. Remember him from Julia's wedding?"

Shane looked about.

"My husband isn't here, Master Hart," Githa said.

"Mister," Shane said.

"I beg your pardon. I thought . . ."

"No. I'm human." His gaze flicked around the table again. "Probably the only human in the lot of you, unless . . ." He looked hopefully at Kris.

"Sorry," Kris said. "Pixie fullblood." He added, comfortingly, "The person who just bolted was human. Do you want us to get him back for you?"

"I do not." Shane's eyes looked as stormy as Queenie had ever seen them.

"Well then . . . I'm pretty sure our waiter is . . ." He wound down as Shane glared at him.

"Dad, you know Gillan, of course," Queenie said.

He nodded.

"Hello, Shane," Gillan said in a friendly voice. "I'd shake your hand, but you see, I have my granddaughter. Isn't she lovely?"

For the first time, Shane's posture softened. He looked at

the baby in Gillan's arms. "She is," he said. He reached over and made the sign of the cross over the baby's head. "God bless and keep you, little one."

Githa gave him an approving look. "Thank you, Mister Hart, "I'm sure He will."

Queenie's heart was beating uncomfortably fast.

She wondered why she had ever thought this was a good idea.

To be fair, she'd known it might go very pear-shaped.

The besom fell against the arm of her chair, and she grasped the handle.

This situation needs a right guid sweeping.

On impulse, she thrust it out, handle first, to Branok.

"What's this, Cousin Queenie? A peace stick?"

"Noo, it's ma besom, thou impertinent wee mun."

Kris looked up from his sketching, his eyes lit with an unholy grin. "Great bogle, Shane—*what* a glorious daughter you have. I have one too . . . and the lord moves in mysterious ways when He gives such wondrous creatures into the care of we mere fathers."

"I'm emancipated," Queenie said.

"I'm sure you are . . . but your dad will love you forever and want to throttle anyone who gets in your way."

Shane spared him a glance. "What's your girl's name?"

"Jisinia. We call her Jin. Here!" He showed Shane the drawing.

Shane nodded and indicated the curly-haired man standing beside her. "What's *he* do?"

"Early childhood teacher. I believe the experience comes in handy when dealing with Jin's less user-friendly moods."

"Queenie's bloke drives a bus and runs a handyman business."

That wasn't quite what Mitch did, but Kris nodded. "Yes, he's in the same line of work as my nephew. Useful lads to have around."

"We're going out to dinner with Queenie's bloke," Shane said.

Kris touched his shoulder gently. "I think your cousin wants to say something . . ."

Shane turned reluctantly to Branok, who had got out of his chair, holding Queenie's besom.

He came around the table and stood by Shane's chair. "Do get up, Shane. I can't stand here all day."

Shane got up. He was half a head taller than Branok.

Branok held out the besom, and Shane said, "What am I meant to do with this?"

"Must you be so *bleddy* literal? You just don't do symbolism, do you?"

"No."

"Well, what about this, then?" Branok shoved the besom back into Queenie's hand and held out his arms. "Cousin Shane, I unreservedly apologise for any hurt or offence I caused you when we were younger. I was a little shit. I was cocky and stubborn and . . . I admired you so much. I don't pretend we'll ever be best friends, but I *would* like to feel that at least we can be civil. For Ma-Ma's sake? She always asks after you."

Shane glanced at Queenie, then he looked into the baby's wondering eyes. His face softened. "Queenie, if you and Mitch make things official, I wouldn't mind one of those . . . only if you want to, of course."

He switched his attention to Branok. "Okay, Bran. While we're baring our souls here . . . I admit I resented you. Everything came so *easily* to you. It all fell into your hands. I had to—"

"You had to work hard for what you have," Gillan put in.

"That's why I so admire you," Branok added. "You and Liberty made a life for yourselves, and you pushed out the boat when you made *her*." He pointed to Queenie. "Or should

I say, *them*."

"I'm a *she*, singular," Queenie said.

Shane nodded. "Yes. Your boys must have done something right too . . ." He smiled briefly at the baby. "What's Mullion up to?"

"Wed with a child as well," Branok said.

"Okay." Shane swallowed. "As far as I'm concerned, we can bury whatever hatchet might be hanging about." He stepped forward and gave his cousin a hug. "You were a thoroughgoing twerp, Bran, but you turned out all right, I guess. Mind you, I was a resentful prick. Not now, though. No reason to be." He cleared his throat. "Lib's at a conference, but we're going out to dinner with Queenie and her bloke. Would you and Gillan like to come? You too, Githa, though I quite understand if you need an early night with Cammie."

She smiled. "Thanks, Mister Hart. Another time, maybe. We're having Cammie baptised on Christmas Eve if you'll be in town? Mull is to be godfather, and Dahlia and Morgana godmothers, but we wanted a sponsor too—and we decided we'd ask the first person who spontaneously blessed our Cammie."

"I'd be honoured," Shane said. He took one of his business cards out of his wallet. "You can call me on this number any time, and either I or Liberty will answer."

Branok patted him on the shoulder. "Thanks, mate."

Queenie thought the colloquialism sounded odd coming from him, but she saw Shane appreciated it.

I'd better call Mitch — and leave a message for Mum.

Shane said to Branok, "Can you suggest a good place for dinner? It's been a while since we were here."

"What kind of place?" Gillan asked. "Café, restaurant . . . pub? We can't come back here . . . they close at five because Flick and Chas have kids and they like to keep their evenings free for them."

"Pub sounds good. Somewhere that does good old-fashioned food."

Branok said, "There's a place called The Pear Tree, but I'd better warn you, it's run by a hob—Adkins Perry."

"They do have good food though," Gillan put in. "Stews, beef and beer pies, glazed ham with baked veg . . . that style of thing."

"Sounds good to me," Shane said, patting his stomach. He reached out for the plate of tarts. "Just one, to leave room for dinner. Oh—" He turned to Queenie. "Will this be okay with Mitch, love? Some of his folk are veggies—right?"

"There are vegetarian options," Gillan said.

Kris got up. "I'd better go, before I start drooling."

"You're welcome to come too, Master Peckerdale," Queenie said.

"I'd like that, but I need to be back. Calypso is dancing at the Cats' Pyjamas tonight and I would hate to miss it. It's our thirty-fifth anniversary and she's promised I can have her in the dressing room, wearing that preposterous costume."

He took Queenie's hand. "You arrange the pick-up with my nephew, Queenie, and I'll be in touch. May I have one of those order forms you gave the gentleman who was in such a hurry?"

Queenie handed him one.

"I'll be in touch about that, too. We—various bits of the family—run a B and B in Patterdale as well as our gallery. I'd love to add some Christmas tarts to the menu."

"I do a big sharing tart called the Cornucopia," Queenie said. "They're not on the form yet."

"Send us a dozen of them. I'll email you about the fix. Peck can do the pick-up. Oh, by the way . . . do you have something with figs? Calypso adores them. We shared figs on our first morning together."

"There will be figs on the Cornucopia."

"Brilliant."

He sauntered out.

Queenie knew that the Cornucopia was not to be the only tart with figs. The tenth Christmas tart had sprung into being in her mind.

The Figgy Pudding . . . packed with spices and a mix of fresh and dried figs, a drop of plum brandy, and a rich and sticky glaze.

Mitch is going to go berserk *for that . . .*

Chapter Eighteen: The Eleventh Tart

Queenie Hart, November — December, 2021

The dinner at the Pear Tree Pub was unexpectedly enjoyable. Shane and Branok conversed in a relaxed manner, and Queenie even saw them laughing over a few of their teenaged exploits.

Liberty and Gillan, after a cordial but consciously polite greeting, settled down to talk about the fine line between helicopter parenting and too much free-range. Nobody could ever have accused Liberty of being a helicopter, but Queenie was glad to see them talking so freely.

She wanted to ask Liberty about Great-Granny Adelaide's painting, which she had left de-framed on the bed, but the chance didn't arise. Anyway, what would Liberty say? She'd advised Queenie to drop it.

The surname, Breck Mulholland, or maybe just Mulholland, must have been Adelaide's maiden name, which made sense if the painting was done before she married Mister Southey. Janet would have been a small child.

Maybe I might show it to Kris sometime . . .

They stayed late over dinner, and when Master Perry finally called time at half-past ten, Mitch reminded Queenie that they could stay overnight with his parents.

To Queenie's surprise, he bypassed the dark farmhouse to spend the night in a barn, filled with sweet-smelling hay and bundles of air-drying herbs.

"No room in the house?" she ventured, settling into the bedding he'd conjured. "Not that this isn't lovely."

"Plenty of room," he said. "But—I have an ambition to eat the Queen of Tarts—that's if you're not too tired?"

"Never," Queenie said.

Mitch brought her quickly to a pitch of writhing and squealing that made her pleased they *hadn't* slept in the house. She clung to him weakly, her heart thumping, as he found his own relief.

When he'd finished he said, "Too much, my lovely?"

"N-no. I just need a minute."

He cuddled her close. "I had a word with your dad tonight while we were getting that order of pears and cheese. Don't worry, I didn't ask for your hand, but I *did* say I very much wanted to marry you. He said it was your affair but for what it was worth, he gave me his blessing. He also gave me your mum's blessing. Apparently she had raised the subject with him already."

"She never mentioned it to me."

"No . . . but Queenie, you and I have talked about it. Will you say yes to me?"

"I think I already have. I'll say yes to James, too, if he asks me."

"He will."

"Aye."

"Next September, then, for me, and October for him?"

"Yes." She sighed. "I wish I could let him know before then rather than present him with a fait accompli. Well—it's not really that, because he *will* know, but he can't respond to the idea."

"We might find a way." He hugged her close. "We'll have to see about a ring."

"And a wedding necklace."

"You already have that."

She touched the thistle gaud. "So I do." She had never intended to wear it every day, but so far she hadn't taken it off since James fastened it at Halloween.

The next morning, Beaman, apparently untroubled that his son and his son's lover had spent the night in the barn, gave Queenie a huge jar of clover honey for her tarts, plus a full comb of the heather honey his wife preferred. He and Danna were unsurprised to hear the wedding plans. Danna seemed to think it had been settled at Halloween when Queenie accepted the gaud.

As soon as she got back to The Belfry, Queenie added the new tarts to her growing list.

"I have eleven," she said to Mitch, looking up from her writing.

"Oh? Regale me."

"Bats in the Belfry — caramel and chocolate. The Ayesha — salmon with lemon. Chess-Nut Tart — antique mince pie filling with chestnut puree. The Fair and Equal — vanilla and caraway and pistachio paste. The Beeman — honey and marzipan. The Queen of Spades — black currant jelly and chocolate. The King of Clubs-black cherry and coffee. The King of Diamonds — red currant and cherry brandy. Lemon Sunshine — rosewater and candied rose petals. The Figgy Pudding — fresh and dried figs with plum brandy glaze."

Mitch stared at her in awe. "And I get to taste all those."

"You definitely do."

"What about the Queen of Hearts?"

"There is the enhanced version of that one, but Oliver specified *new,* so I think I might keep that as a bonus. The Kings and Queens are the simplest."

"Two more to go, then," he said.

"No — one. I thought of a new one last night. The Pear Tree, in honour of the pub. That one is going to have poached pears in quince jelly, and a tree made of chocolate and angelica."

Mitch said, "As I said before, this will be an expensive set of tarts."

"Since it pays my rent for a whole year . . ."

"There is that. What happens next year? Do you have to come up with twelve new ones?"

She laughed and shook her head. "No, Oliver said *next* year's rent is to be twelve tarts of his choosing. He reckons by then he'll have a good impression of the possibilities." She added, "I'll send him an extra dozen of some little ones with rainbow sprinkles, because he loves to share them with Kit and Pascoe—Andy and Dellion's little boys. I don't think tarts containing black chocolate and brandy would be suitable for them."

"They're suitable for me though," Mitch hinted.

"Aye, thou glutton. I'm also going to make a giant family tart with twelve slices . . . I'll use the Queen of Hearts in that one because the Ayesha might not quite fit in."

Oops, I meant to keep that one as a surprise.

She gave a mental shrug and added, "I'm also making twelve variants of shortbread."

"James will like that."

"I hope so." She thought of James. It was almost two months since she had seen him. Lassie Haggis stirred, wanting her bagpipe music, wanting her laddie, longing to have him in his kilt.

No' noo, lassie. When the wee beasties are near.

She went to her bedroom, intending to restore the painting to the frame, but Mitch had done it already.

Of course—he's The Fixer.

The next three weeks were packed with activity. The Chess-Nuts' party was just the first of many Christmas festivities, and also the first public appearance for Queenie's mince pies . . .made in the modern sense of fruit without the beef.

Queenie was rushed almost off her feet as new orders came in daily.

Kris Peckerdale and Flick Dark both ordered tarts for their December guests—not the specials Queenie was making for Oliver, but some of her existing recipes, topped with marzipan stars and Christmas trees for a festive touch.

An order came in from Martha Farnham, the bank manager's wife, and one for two dozen shortbread from a woman named Penny Bunn. Queenie thought that was a joke until she recalled Liberty's original name had been Liberty Bell. A second look showed her the address at Mother Goose Lane. Ms Bunn must be the woman who had taken over her unit.

Fortunately, shortbread was less perishable than tarts, so she was able to send some of her orders in the post, or via Mitch and Ethel.

Kris Peckerdale had finished painting her van. She was delighted with the effect, which was both rich and tasteful. He'd included her website.

Duncan Dee went on stocking some of her tarts in his deli, and Oakengrove put in a big order for their community Christmas party.

Queenie installed a bigger freezer, trying to get ahead.

She saw less of Mitch than she wanted, because he was so busy too, but surely January would offer more free time.

On the eighteenth of December, someone knocked on The Belfry door.

Queenie stuck her head out, blinking in bright sunlight.

For a moment she didn't recognise the young woman standing on the top step. She was blonde with delicate features and quite a lot of silver jewellery.

"Greet you," she said, since the girl was obviously fay.

"And you, Queenie. I came to see if you could let us have some shortbread for the christening."

"The—oh! Come in, Githa."

"I will. Is Mitchell here?"

"Yes—for once. He'd up in the belltower with Ayesha. That's his cat," she added helpfully.

"Zen needs to see him." She turned and hollered, in a surprisingly loud voice, "Zenn-or!"

"Here!" Zennor St Ives came around the corner of The Belfry.

Queenie hadn't seen him in years, but she thought she would have recognised him from his likeness to his parents. He was handsome, with the black silky hair she remembered and delft-blue eyes. He came up and gave her a friendly smile, with just a hint of something odd in it.

Queenie was alarmed to feel Lassie Haggis stirring again. She wanted her besom.

"Hello, Zen," she said, as evenly as she could.

"Cousin Queenie. My word, you've changed."

"Ye havenae."

"Oh?" His brows went up and he stepped closer. "Oho! What have we here?"

Githa laid her hand on his arm. "Zen, stop that. Queenie says Mitchell is in the belltower, so why don't you go up and see him . . . and his cat?"

"I'm not afraid of cats."

"Did I say you were?"

Zen gave her a quick kiss on the ear, and she smiled delightedly. "Later."

"Through that door and up the stairs," Queenie said, wondering at the byplay.

When Zennor had vanished, Githa said, "I could have made the order through your website, but I had to see you."

"Come on in for a cup of tea," Queenie said.

The pisky woman followed her to the kitchen, expressing admiration for The Belfry while Queenie put the jug on to boil.

"I have to speak with you about a dog," she said abruptly, seating herself.

"What dog?" Queenie was puzzled. It was about the last thing she'd expected.

Githa leaned forward. "You obviously know Gillan pretty well. She's my mother-by-love."

"Yes."

"And you also know Lady Velvet. She's *not* my mother-by-love, because that would just be — weird."

"I suppose it would."

Githa opened a shoulder bag she was carrying and pulled out a document folder. She opened it and passed it to Queenie.

Queenie saw it contained two coloured photocopies of framed paintings. One depicted an enchanting little silver-grey hound, and the other a smooth-haired dachshund — chocolate brown. He — it was obviously a *he* — had blue eyes, and each whisker and brow hair was perfectly defined.

"They're lovely. Are they yours?" Queenie asked.

Githa said, "Tamzin from Elf-Made Art did the first one for Zen, and he got a matching one done after he met me."

Queenie had meant to ask if the dogs were Githa's, but she let it go.

Githa pointed to the hound. "This is Guinevere. The other one is Demi-Dog."

"Good names."

"We think so." Githa looked at her hopefully.

Queenie poured boiling water over the tea. A client named Jack Miller had given her a tea set painted with holly after she'd made some rosewater shortbread especially for his wife.

The set was fine and beautiful, but she hadn't realised *how* fine a gift it was until Maureen Tucker of the *Stradevarious* had pointed out that it was a Jonathan Blarney original and thus one of a kind.

She said, "Githa, I'm probably being dense, but I seem to be missing something. "

"I'm making a mess of this," Githa said. "Um . . ." She clasped her hands in her lap and looked down at them, twisting the silver ring on her wedding finger.

A sudden yowl from the belltower made Queenie freeze, but there was no corresponding yell, so she just had to hope Ayesha hadn't damaged Zen St Ives.

Wheesht moggy! He's a gey irritating laddie but he does no' deserve to be mangled.

She took down two holly-wreathed cups, and hesitated. "Githa, will Zen want a cup of tea?"

The girl didn't answer, so she turned to repeat it.

Githa had gone, but a dainty silvery hound, surely the one from the picture, sat by the chair. She thumped her tail on the floor and flattened her ears at Queenie.

Queenie wanted to pat the lovely thing, but a memory of Lady Velvet prevented her. This hound wasn't like the dignified black spaniel bitch who was Gillan's second self, but she had the same aura of *otherness.*

Queenie sat down, keeping her gaze on the hound.

"Guinevere, I assume," she said softly.

Guinevere got up and came to lay her head on Queenie's knee, so maybe patting would be okay. She stroked the little dog's head.

After a minute or so, the hound dissolved into the young woman, kneeling with her head bowed.

Queenie lifted her hand away.

This is so weird.

Weirder than kissing your laddie and having him turn into your pixie man in your arms?

Githa shook her head as if waking, then she got fluidly to her feet and sat back down in her chair.

"I *see*," Queenie said.

"Yes. And Demi is Zen's mani-dog. He's not terribly

substantial, but—" She shrugged.

"Both of you. What about—" She juggled names in her head and remembered. "What about Camelot?"

"We don't know, yet, but it seems—likely." Githa smoothed her hair. "Muties like us aren't very common, and it's practically unheard of for two of us to marry and to be compatible. No one has ever identified the mutie gene—if it is a gene—so we really *don't* know if Cammie will have a mani-self or not. Obviously, it doesn't matter if she hasn't one. We're not *trying* to breed muties."

Queenie got up again and poured the tea, absently shifting her besom away from the kitchen bench. It had developed a mind of its own since her afternoon tea at the Dark Room. "It's verra interesting, but I'm no' sure wha' it has to do wi' mysel'," she said.

Githa said, "Nothing, really. I was just taking a short cut. Zen and I have done a bit of research, because a maid Zen knows—the artist he regards as a foster sister, before you start wondering—once asked *very* tactfully if Demi and Guinny could have pups together. We plain didn't know, so, as I said—a bit of research. We didn't learn anything that pertains to *us,* but we did find out something we definitely weren't expecting. *We* are people—piskies—with dog mani-selves and I asked Zen once, just in fun, if he thought there were any dogs out there who had *people* mani-selves."

Queenie felt her jaw drop.

"Yes, that's the way Zen looked, too. He said he bleddy well hoped not, and I can see his point. It seems there aren't. At least, we haven't found even a hint of it. You'll never guess what we did find, though. There's a strain of hounds—tough, long-lived little beasts—and I mean, *really* long-lived little beasts. Forty or fifty years is not uncommon. They're *not* mani-selves, but they age in the same way, though they're born as puppies rather than just—emerging, the way Guinny and Demi-Dog did."

Queenie stared at her.

Githa went on, "You know a woman named Mevrouw van Zijl, I believe?"

At least this was sure ground, and Queenie grasped it with relief. "Yes . . . she's one of the Chess-Nut club members. She's also one of my clients, and an old friend of Danna . . . Mitch's mum."

"I know. She's kanaalfee."

"I know that, too. What about her? Is she a friend of yours?"

"I wouldn't say that. No. Friends don't put compulsions on other friends."

Compulsions? Queenie itched for her *Fay Companion,* her go-to encyclopaedia of all things fay.

If I could only conjure I'd have it in my hand.

Githa went on, "She's the one who laid it on me to speak to you because she thought a long-lived dog would be of *personal* interest to you." Githa smoothed her hair again and cocked her head. For a moment Queenie almost saw the pretty hound again peering out of bright pisky eyes. "I don't know why she asked me to tell you this . . . but now I have." She blew out her cheeks and shook her head again.

"Are you okay, Githa?" Queenie asked. She put a cup of tea in front of her guest.

"Yes. Just a bit lightheaded. The compulsion. Ugh." She frowned, got up and shook herself like a wet dog. She sat down again and then she added, brightly, "All gone now."

"What on earth is a compulsion?"

"Oh . . . it's like influence, but more so. Zen uses influence sometimes, but when he does it you just feel a little bit more likely to let him have what he wants. He used to use it to pick up information. Not that he ever did anything with it. He just liked to *know*. Information gathering and hoarding is a pisky trait."

Queenie remembered Branok telling her that back in August when she first went to his office. That trait had worked emphatically to her advantage, since Branok wanted to know about her Caledonian Curse.

"Zen doesn't do it with *me*, but then, why would he? I want what he wants anyway — and vice versa. I'll always tell him what's on my mind unless it's not his business in which case he won't ask." She sipped her tea. "His mum just about had him trained before I got my paws on him. Apparently, she threatened him with castor oil in his coffee if he *ever* used influence where it wasn't warranted. She'd do it, too."

Queenie didn't doubt it.

"Compulsions, though." Githa sipped again. "This is wonderful tea and I love the cup. So pretty."

"Compulsions?"

"Hmm. More like a shove. Imagine a toy boat. You blow on it, gently and it eases away from the edge of the pool. That's influence. You give it a good push. It shoots forward until the push dissipates, and it might almost get swamped. That's a compulsion. I wasn't terribly pleased when Mevrouw van Zijl put one on me. It was just a mild one, and it's gone now, but *still*."

Queenie's head was spinning still. She said, "But *why* use you to tell me about dogs? She could easily have told me herself."

"She didn't want you to think she's interfering . . . wouldn't want it to get back to Mistress Kingsolver."

"But I know the info came from her now, anyway," Queenie pointed out.

The pisky girl narrowed her eyes. "So you do. I must have let that piece of intelligence slip. Oops."

"Weel, ma tricky wee bitchie, I'll take guid care never to cross ye!" Queenie said.

Githa looked startled, then she gave her sweet smile. "Very

wise, dear Queenie. I'm a nice person, mostly, given that I'm a pisky, but if you cross me I get *cross,* and bitchiness is an inevitable part of my nature."

She picked up her tea again. "Thanks for this. I get quite thirsty these days. Suckling a baby does that. Speaking of whom, I need to get back to her soon. *She* gets cross if she doesn't get her milk right now this second when she wants it, and she makes her feelings known. Takes after her dad.

"By the way, if you should be interested in a heather-hound puppy, there's a litter planned for August next year. The little beasts will be ready for their new homes in October. I should put your name down *now,* because . . . they like to choose their people, and besides, the pups are usually re-served a long while ahead."

Queenie decided her brain would just have to accept it. She said, "Thank you for the information, although I'm sorry you felt you *had* to tell me. Mitch and I were discussing getting a dog."

"I'll give you the contact. No phone or email — the breeder is a halfling living *over there.*" She grimaced. "The ridiculous thing is — if Mevrouw van Zjil had simply *asked* me, I'd have happily told you. I like people to be happy . . . and little dogs, obviously. There was *no* need for her ridiculous compulsion. Are you going to tell her I dropped her in it?"

"Probably not."

"Only *probably?*"

"I won't, but Lassie Haggis just might, if she gets riled enough."

Githa giggled. "*Tricky wee bitchie* indeed. Something tells me you're another maid it doesn't *do* to cross. Let's be friends."

"Let's," Queenie said.

Githa gave a pleased little wriggle. She conjured a bit of paper, wrote an address, and handed it to Queenie. "The

Hoond House. Yes, really, what's what they call it. Now, about that shortbread?"

Queenie quite forgot to ask again if Zennor wanted some tea, but it didn't matter, because two minutes after the order for the christening was finalised, the men came out of the belltower, with Ayesha riding on Mitch's shoulder.

Zen glanced at Queenie and then he reminded Githa that they'd better get back to Gillan and Branok's place to reclaim their daughter.

After they'd gone, Mitch put Ayesha down on the floor, and she stalked over to the spot where Guinevere had been sitting. She sniffed several times, and then she sneezed.

Mitch poured himself some tea. "Did you have a good visit with Githa, my love?" he asked.

"Yes. Sort of. She's a very *odd* girl."

"People with manis often are."

"You knew about her? That she's a mutie?"

"I didn't before today . . . well, I hadn't met her until five minutes ago."

"That's right. She didn't come to the Pear Tree dinner."

He continued, "I didn't know Zennor was one either."

"Obviously you do now."

Mitch said, "Yes. He showed me. Scared the bejeezus out of Ayesha. He — the little mani-dog — sniffed her and she took umbrage and made a roundhouse swipe at him."

That would be the yowl I heard.

"I hope she didn't hurt him too much."

"Not a bit. Her claws went straight through him. You should have seen her face!"

"What did Zen want to see you about? Surely, not just to demonstrate his mutie skills."

"It's Fixer business."

"Oh. Everything okay?"

"Not sure yet. I have hopes." He sipped his tea, put down the cup, pulled his phone out and put it away again.

Queenie felt a touch of unease.

He's got the fidgets.

She reached for her besom.

Mitch caught her eye and said quickly, "Queenie, remember Oliver saying something about polishing the bells?"

"Yes. I feel a bit guilty about that, but I've hardly had time to start a big job . . .I assume it will be a big job?"

"I thought we might do it together . . . maybe an hour each evening. That's if you'd want to."

"I would."

"Then let's start tonight."

CHAPTER NINETEEN: THE BELLS

Queenie Hart, December, 2021

Polishing Kerensa Porthwellian's bells made an oasis of peace for Queenie and Mitch in the week leading up to Christmas.

Oliver had cleared the belltower after the bats' departure, and it had become Ayesha's domain, but Queenie hadn't spent a lot of time there. It was on her to-do list.

Mitch made the place inviting by conjuring in a low couch and a table where they could have supper.

The belltower room was round, as might be expected, and it had a long horizontal window, invisible from the ground. This ran right around, giving a panoramic view of Kirk Circle, the old rectory grounds, and the graveyard. It had shutters, operated via a lever, and Queenie supposed Oliver must have installed it for the bats' convenience.

Kerensa's bells hung in a cluster of seven, close together, but somehow arranged so each could swing independently and freely. Their ropes were neatly bundled, to keep them out of the way.

Queenie examined the bells. Each was slightly different in size, and each had a name incised into the bronze.

She read them out in turn. "Loveday, Honour . . ." She paused.

"Obey?" Mitch asked from where he was preparing the polish.

"No. Hope. Joy, Contentment, Justice and . . ." She got up

151

on her toes, to read the final name. "Truth."

Mitch left the polish and came to put his arms around her. "Not a bad recipe for life, my darling love."

"No' bad at all."

He stood back and conjured two soft rags.

Queenie looked at them suspiciously. "I hope these are not—"

"No, beloved, they're not. Can't have bell polish getting on your coochie."

She laughed. "Jam is bad enough."

"Let's start with Loveday."

Mitch tipped a small amount of polish onto his rag. It smelled surprisingly agreeable.

"Dad makes this," he said. "It has beeswax in it." He glanced at Ayesha, who was resting in her music stool bed. "It doesn't even make Mistress Spit-Spat sneeze."

"No' so much o' the spit-spat these days," Queenie observed. She remembered the yowl that had recently echoed forth from the tower, but she supposed any cat might be excused that when her admonitory box to an impertinent dog's ears had encountered thin air.

She followed suit with the polish, and she found it oddly satisfying to wipe it on, let it dry, then rub it clean. The bronze came up to a magical gleam.

Mitch undid the bell rope and tugged. Loveday swung in a smooth arc, releasing a high tingggg.

"She's a tenor," Mitch said.

The sound reverberated around the room and Queenie listened, rapt, until it faded into the stonework.

One bell down. Six to go.

She sat down to enjoy the ambience of the belltower. The one gleaming bell reminded her of the strangeness of the weeks leading up to Halloween, when the bells had reacted to the restless bats with a not-quite audible hum.

Jamie helped me through it.

She pictured James in his ridiculous argyle sweater, and his even more ridiculous tartan pyjamas.

"What are you smiling about, my love?"

"I wa' thinkin' o' ma laddie . . . he tried to shower in tartan pyjamas."

Mitch shuddered. "Thank you for that picture, my own love. It will haunt me."

Queenie held out her arms. "Shall we?" She had an urge to make love in the belltower.

"We shall not. Madam Spit-Spat would object."

"I suppose so." Queenie put away the idea. "We can have supper here, though."

"I'll fetch it."

He went down to fetch their prepared meal, and Queenie relaxed.

"Moggy?"

There was no answering mew.

She must ha' gone doon.

Bell by bell, and evening by evening, Kerensa's bells were transformed. Bell by bell, they gave out their songs, from the high and mellow *tinggg* of Loveday to the deep tolling of Justice.

Busy as that time was, Queenie relished it. There was something magical about Christmas—the first she'd ever spent with her lover.

One small problem remained . . . she'd hadn't yet come up with a twelfth tart for Oliver's Twelve Tarts of Christmas rent payment.

"I could just make up a recipe, but all the others have represented something special to me—something happening in my life," she said to Mitch. "The bats in my dear Belfry, Ayesha accepting me . . ."

"Me finally being able to accept James."

"The roses you brought me to celebrate the Citrus."

"The Chess-Nuts party . . ."

Queenie sighed. She wasn't sure how she felt about the Chess-Nuts now, since learning of Githa's experience with Mevrouw van Zijl. "I could do something for the thistle gaud, maybe . . . but I already have thistle in the Fair and Equal."

"Never mind . . . something will come to you," Mitch said.

"I expect so." She hoped so. Time was getting short.

Chapter Twenty: The Twelfth Tart

Queenie Hart, Christmas Eve, December, 2021

Queenie and Mitch polished the final bell, the deep-toned Justice, on Christmas Eve.

They were admiring the effect when Queenie heard a knock on the door.

"Whoever is that?"

"I'll go." Mitch kissed her affectionately. He picked up Ayesha from her accustomed seat and carried her down the stairs.

Queenie leaned back on the couch. She heard voices below.

"Are you sure you want to do this?"

She frowned. Who on earth was that? The voice was somewhat familiar. *Dad*? She'd seen Shane that morning, when they all attended the christening of little Camelot Morgana St Ives.

The trip to Sydney had taken time she could ill afford, but she *couldn't* not go. She owed a lot to Branok and Gillan, and her dad had been so proud and happy to be invited as Camelot's senior sponsor.

Seeing him holding the little girl had given Queenie a sudden flash of how he might have been with her . . . and how he might be when she had children.

She'd been pleased to meet the priest, too . . . a dark-eyed young man with an operatic singing voice which he had used to grand effect as he sang baby Camelot into the comfort and joy of her new family.

Dai Daffyd, his name was, and he was going to marry her to Mitch in September. It seemed a long time to wait.

Longer for me and Jamie.

She supposed Shane *might* have come to call, but hadn't he been going off to the Pear Tree with Branok?

Liberty was visiting Gillan — but wait, weren't the St Iveses hosting a large gathering for Christmas?

Maybe Mum and Dad will come here to us tomorrow. I can show Mum Adelaide's painting.

"If you're sure, Mitchell."

Not Dad. Who, then? Branok? Their voices have the same timbre.

"I'm sure." That was Mitch, sounding apprehensive.

Queenie wanted to go downstairs and find out who, and what, was causing her pixie man unease.

Then came utter silence.

She touched her ears.

That's a glamour.

Mitch and James had both brought silence when she'd needed it.

She drew in a breath, quieting herself.

It's all right. Fixer business. Obviously, he won't want me learning the details of someone else's private pain.

She lay back, gazing at the bells.

Loveday, Honour, Hope, Joy, Contentment, Justice, Truth.

A good recipe for life. A wonderful thought for Christmas.

The quiet continued.

The lantern which Mitch lit every evening in the belltower dimmed.

It must be getting late.

A door closed downstairs.

Finally!

She meant to sit up, to call Mitch, but a languor came over her.

Tinggggg

She opened her eyes.

Loveday is calling.

She heard feet on the steps, and someone came into the belltower. The soft scent of wool bathed her senses and she smiled.

"Jamie."

"My dearie."

She sat up and reached out her arms. "Come here and gie' me a wee smooch."

James smiled down at her. He was dressed in his kilt. He was heartbreakingly beautiful, but he was no mere memory. He was warm and he was solid. He sat beside her and settled into her arms.

"It's gey guid to see ye, laddie . . . but it's no' October."

He laughed. "No, but — this is a Christmas gift."

She kissed him. "How? From whom?"

"Never mind how. We don't have long. Oh, Queenie, I love you so much."

"And I loe ye, laddie." She caught herself and added, "I mean, *I* love you. Lassie Haggis does, always did, but *I* love you . . . when I'm myself."

"I'm glad."

Tonggggg

"What the devil is that?"

"It's Hope. One of Kerensa's bells."

"Of course it is. My memories are still . . ."

She kissed him again. "Jamie, can you get naked?"

"I thought you wanted me in my kilt?"

"Love the kilt, but please . . ."

He freed one hand and he kissed his fingers. The kilt vanished, but the scent of clean wool remained.

"Do mine. I give you permission."

He kissed his fingers again, then he gathered her close.

"Hot and hard?" she asked.

"Need you ask — hurry!" He laughed, breathlessly.

Queenie rolled on her side, and James came down to join

her, sliding in.

"Ooh, slippery," he said.

Queenie sucked on his lower lip. "Hard."

He pressed in, skilled and certain as Mitch, but nothing like him.

Dinnnnng.

Joy sang out.

James gathered her closer. "Queenie, my lassie, my dearie, my love . . . will you be my wife?"

"I will! Will the first day of October do for the wedding?"

"Aye . . . you'll need to make the arrangements."

"I know. Are you nearly there? Because I —" A squeal burst from her as Honour sounded with her full and certain note.

James gathered himself. He thrust in hard and collapsed against her. "Oh, glory, glory . . ." His voice broke.

"Hallelujah?" Queenie asked.

James gasped and spluttered. "Trust you to lower the tone, my darling lassie. Is she there, by the way?"

"Aye, here, I am, ye windbag . . . hot in the coochie for ye."

"But we just —"

Queenie said, urgently, "Go again?"

"Yes . . ."

Justice boomed.

James kissed her fiercely, and Lassie Haggis laughed. She wanted her besom to wave like a wand to keep this moment forever.

The waves broke over them again as Contentment gave her sweet voice.

Just one more.

James, perspiring with effort, his eyes glowing in full heather, sat up. "I have something — is my childhood basket still in the kitchen?"

"No, it's by my chest near the bed," she said, puzzled.

He kissed his fingers.

The small carved wooden box landed in his hand, and he

laid his fingers on it and opened the lid.

I never knew that opened.

"Ring for you," he said, his eyes flaring. "Quick!"

Queenie held out her hand.

"Right hand . . . here's mine . . . oh, hurry!"

He dropped a large ring into her palm. "Together now . . . and we say . . ."

The words came into her head.

"I know, laddie . . . I read aboot it in ma wee book."

"Now," James said.

Together, they said *I betroth thee* as the plain red gold rings slid into place.

Truth sang her impossibly high sweet note into the night.

Then — the whole peal rang as midnight sounded.

Queenie kissed her betrothed and clung to him. "I love you, my Jamie."

He laughed. "I'll see you on our wedding day, dearie. Merry —" His voice faded, and other arms were about Queenie.

"Christmas," Mitch said. He gave Queenie a hug and then leaned back to look at her ruefully. "Sorry, my darling love. That was all we could manage."

"All . . . we . . ."

A soft blanket fell over Queenie, and she started to sit up.

"No, stay there. It's okay."

"Hello?" An uncertain voice sounded from the head of the stair.

Mitch said, "Come in, Zen. We're decent."

The lights came up, and Zennor St Ives stepped into the belltower. He removed the blanket from Ayesha's throne, put on the seat, and sat down.

"Greet you, Queenie," he said.

Queenie found her besom to hand. "Wha' are *ye* doin' here?"

Zennor made patting motions in the air. "I'm here by

arrangement, Cousin Queenie. Do settle down. I'm a married man, and you're my cousin. I do *not* want to see your assets . . ."

Queenie dragged herself into order and the blanket up to her neck. It was the one from James' basket, she noted. "What on earth is going on?" she asked.

Zen said, "I'll be off now, Mitchell. I just stayed to make sure you were okay. You're . . ."

"I'm fine. Thanks, Zen. I owe you."

Zen said, "No problem. Just *don't* tell Ma. I don't like the taste of castor oil. Goodnight, and Merry Christmas."

He walked off down the stairs.

Mitch lay back, and then he pushed the blanket down and kissed Queenie's shoulder. "So, you're betrothed to your laddie."

"I am." Queenie lifted her right hand.

"And now—will you accept a ring from me as well?"

"Don't tell me—you have one in a box too?"

"No. I have a pair in my pocket. I wanted to give James a chance to go first . . . mind you, it took some doing. Your young cousin casts a mean influence. And before you ask, my love, it's not something we can do often . . . maybe once a month at most. I'm sorry, but the headache is coming in."

"Use your mum's marigold sovereign."

"I will. Before I do though—" He double-tapped his wrist and caught two rings out of the air—the same as the pair James had, but of a lighter colour. "White gold," he said. "Ready?"

"Ready." Queenie held out her hand.

"I betroth thee."

Two rings shone side by side on her right hand.

And suddenly, on Christmas morning, with just hours before she needed to pay her rent to Oliver, the twelfth tart popped into Queenie's head. It was not the Tart of Kerensa's Bells, although that would come one day as a sharing tart. It was not a Tart of Betrothal, because onion rings . . .

Oh, dear . . .

It was the Merry Christmas, and it would be stuffed with fruit and wear a wreath of holly . . . made of marzipan and smelling of brandy butter.

Queenie sighed. "We'd better go down to bed, darling Mitch. I'll rub some marigold sovereign into your head."

"Yes please, and then I'll put my head on your bosom. That will make me feel better . . ."

Queenie smiled. "Oh, I forgot to tell you. Next October, we're getting a dog . . . a heather-hound . . ."

Mitch said, "What's that? Will Madam Spit-Spat be displeased?"

"It's a verra special dog. Madam Spit-Spat will be visiting your mum when it comes, and *Fair and Equal* is not *only* a tart. Oh, *Mitch*. I'm so happy I could sing."

She didn't quite, but as they walked down the steep steps from the belltower, the seven bells hummed, ever so softly, in The Belfry.

ABOUT THE AUTHOR

Lark Westerly loves creating worlds, and the world of the Fairy in the Bed, Queen of Tarts and Being Tamzin series is one of her all-time favourites.

Research is always a pleasure, and for this story, Lark dug into church bells, vans, roses, and ancient recipes. It was a lot of fun.

Apart from writing, Lark loves walking with her dogs — not heather-hounds but Jack Russell terriers. She enjoys music and cooking, although she has never made a tart in her life. She is married to *one* husband, who has one self only, and she has two children and two grandchildren. For more about Lark and her stories visit her website at https://larksinger.weebly.com

www.ingramcontent.com/pod-product-compliance
Lightning Source LLC
Chambersburg PA
CBHW060822120626
46557CB00001B/331